The Bard of Biology

Adventures in Reason

Kris Langman

Post Hoc Publishing

Chapter One

———◆●◆———

The Tournament

NIKKI SWORE AS her mask slipped over her eyes. She stopped to adjust it. Little ten-year-old Curio, who was walking behind her, bumped into her.

"Sorry, Miss," said Curio, backing up into a row of rustling corn stalks. "It must be a bother having to wear that."

Nikki blinked as bright sunlight streamed into her mask's eyeholes again. "It's more than a bother. It's hot and itchy and it keeps slipping over my eyes. You're lucky you don't have to wear this getup."

She waved her hands vaguely over herself from head to foot. She was wearing not only a mask but also a hooded cloak and a floor-length robe, all made of rough white linen. It was the style of clothing worn by a local cult called the Seekers. The Seekers believed that sunlight on the skin poisoned the mind, or some such nonsense. Nikki hadn't really paid much attention to the Prince's description of the cult. Its members were apparently a common sight in the city of Kingston, so the Prince had decided their style of dress would be an ideal disguise for Nikki. The palace guards were searching for her everywhere, so hiding her face was the only way she could move about freely in public.

Nikki swore again as she tripped over her robe. In their hasty flight from the Southern Castle there'd been no time to adjust the

1

robe's length. She held it up with one hand while holding her mask with the other. Her rucksack was strapped to her back under the hooded cloak and she could feel the rucksack squirming. Not to mention growling. Cation was not happy. She felt a tiny paw swat at her neck. Reaching awkwardly under the cloak she nudged the kitten back down into the depths of the rucksack. "Where exactly are we going?" she asked Athena, who was stumbling along a ploughed furrow in the corn field a few feet ahead. The imp was also dressed as a Seeker, and her short stature made her look like a young child converted to the cult.

"We are headed for the King's tournament, Miss," said Athena. "Most of the people in Kingston will be headed there today. It is a very special event and is very popular. By noontime there will be few people left in the city. Everyone will be out at the fairgrounds. It is the Prince's opinion that Miss Gwendolyn will head for the tournament also, once she notices how empty the city is becoming. It will be safer for her to stay with the crowds."

"I guess that's as good a plan as any," said Nikki.

"Will you two keep it down?" hissed Fuzz, who was leading the way. He was having less trouble walking than the others, as his robe and cloak were a bit too short for him. His dusty leather boots and woolen trousers could be seen beneath the hem of the cloak. "There could be palace guards all over this corn field."

Athena sniffed. "That is highly doubtful. If those ridiculous guards with all their clumsy armor were trampling through the corn they would be making a noise like stampeding buffalo."

"Yeah, well, keep it down anyway," grumbled Fuzz. "You two don't sound anything like typical Seekers. I've met a few on my visits to Kingston, and believe me, they are just about the dumbest people in the Realm. They can barely string two words together. All they do is mumble about things they call spirit beings and how these beings are always whispering stuff into their ears. You wouldn't believe how many of them drown each year. They wander around, listening to the voices in their heads, and walk straight off the Kingston cliffs. The local fishermen find one of them tangled in their herring nets every few months. It's enough to make you swear off fish dinners."

Athena impatiently waved him to silence. They had reached the edge of the corn field. In front of them stretched a wide open area of grassy pastureland. A herd of cows clustered near the corn stalks. The cows were nervously eyeing a long row of canvas tents which had invaded their pasture. Hundreds of people were milling around the tents, with more pouring into the field every second. Most of the tents had tables set up in front of them with things for sale. The baker and brewer tents had the longest lines. People jostled to buy cherry tarts and foaming tankards of ale. In one corner of the field children were flying kites made of crimson silk. The kites swooped and dived like giant birds. Just beyond the kites in a large area of trampled grass men were wrestling and fighting with clanking swords. Each fighter was surrounded by a crowd of gamblers waving money and shouting loudly at their chosen contestants.

"We will separate," whispered Athena. Fuzz immediately started to protest but she dismissed him with a wave of her hand. "It is not ideal, but we will search much faster that way. We all know what Miss Gwendolyn looks like, but remember, she may be in disguise. The palace guards are undoubtedly searching for her." She pointed to four different sections of the pasture. "I will take the area over by the kites. Fuzz, you take the wrestlers. Curio, you take that area bordering the woods, and Miss, you take the area where the tents are. We will meet back here in the cornfield in two hours."

Nikki automatically looked down at her wrist, where the faint tan-line from her watch was still visible. She hadn't been wearing it when Fuzz and Athena brought her through the portal at her high school. She'd never seen a watch here in the Realm of Reason. There'd been a sundial in Deceptionville, but that was the only kind of time-keeping device she'd ever seen in the Realm. "How will we know when two hours are up?" she whispered.

Athena pointed back toward Kingston, where the towers of the Southern Castle loomed dark against the morning sun. "It is now about eight o'clock in the morning, Miss. Watch the sun. When it is just above the tallest tower in the castle it will be ten o'clock."

Nikki nodded and reluctantly stepped out from the cover of the corn stalks. She watched as the other three disappeared into the crowd. She was temporarily alone in the Realm of Reason again and the familiar feeling of anxiety crept over her. She hitched up her robe and tried to focus on her mission. Find Gwen.

As she stumbled across the rutted grass of the pasture her first thought was to look for someone dressed as a Seeker. It was a handy disguise and there were several of the hooded figures about. She eyed them as they passed, but none seemed to match Gwen's height or slender build. Also, just like Fuzz had said, they were all mumbling to themselves. She could imagine Gwen using the Seeker robes as a disguise, but it seemed unlikely that she'd try to copy their mumbling. It was a bright sunny day and most of the tournament-goers were not wearing hoods or cloaks. Gwen couldn't just throw a hood over her pale blond hair, not without people wondering why she was over-dressed for the hot weather. Maybe she'd found a way to dye her hair? As Nikki mulled this over her attention was caught by gasps coming from a tent nearby. She edged through the throng.

A wooden table set up in front of the tent held a collection of ob-jects which immediately reminded her of her freshman physics class. On top of a blue velvet cloth lay two glass rods about a foot in length. Next to the rods was a wooden structure about a foot tall, with a string hanging from it. An elderly man dressed in a shiny gold robe picked up one of the glass rods. He waved it dramatically over his head then rubbed it vigorously with a piece of silk. He tied the glass rod onto the piece of string so that it swung freely in the air. Then he rubbed the other glass rod with the silk. He held the second rod close to the first one, careful not to let them touch. The crowd gasped as the glass rod on the string swung away from the other rod as if pushed by invisible hands.

The electrostatic force, thought Nikki. She'd done this very same experiment in her physics class. When the glass rod was rubbed with silk some of the rod's electrons were transferred to the piece of silk. Since electrons were negative, losing some of them left the glass rod with a positive charge. Since the other glass rod also had a positive charge the two rods repelled each other, causing them to move away from each other as if by magic. The technical term for it was electrostatic repulsion. Same charges repelled, opposite charges attracted.

A small boy clutched the edge of the table, hopping up and down excitedly. "What's making it move? Huh? What's making it?"

The man standing next to him smiled and put a restraining hand on the boy's head. "Careful now, son. You'll scare 'em away."

"Scare who away, Pa? Who? Who?"

"The sprites, of course," said the man. "Them as what's making the rods move." He pulled a coin out of his trouser pocket and tossed it into a little box on the table.

The elderly man in the gold robe made him a formal little bow. He scooped up the coin in his liver-spotted hand and tucked it into a pouch at his waist.

"Sprites, Father? But how cum I can't see 'em? Can you see 'em? Do they have wings? How do you know they're there? Huh? How?"

The boy poked a curious finger into the space between the two rods, but withdrew it hastily when the old man glared at him.

"I know them sprites are there cuz the rods are moving, ain't they?" said the boy's father. "Don't be wasting time with daft questions."

The man led his son away and Nikki stared thoughtfully after them. It was strange, she thought. When people in the Realm of

Reason didn't understand something they invented invisible beings just like people in her own world did. It was as if they thought the entire world was controlled by these imaginary beings. People in her own world had started to move past that kind of thinking about three-hundred years ago, with the start of the scientific revolution. They had started to examine nature more honestly and rigorously, instead of just making up wild stories about magic and invisible spirits. The Realm of Reason, on the other hand, seemed to be stuck firmly in the invisible-being stage. She wondered if it would ever start to move away from that kind of superstition. It was a long and difficult process, and it seemed to require a few brave and inventive people to kick it off. In her world it had been people like Galileo, Newton, and Leonardo da Vinci, who had been not only an artist but also an engineer and naturalist, famous for his anatomically accurate drawings of people, animals, and insects. Here in the Realm of Reason some of its citizens had begun to take small steps down that path. Gwen, for one, and the Prince of Physics, for another. Athena and Curio also seemed headed in that direction, though they didn't do experiments the way Gwen and the Prince did. They were just open-minded and curious and willing to evaluate evidence. Even Kira, an uneducated sailor, had started down the path of reason due to her expertise in navigation. Perhaps there was hope for the Realm yet.

"Hey! You. Yes, I'm talking to you, Missy."

Nikki jumped. The old man in the gold robe was waving his finger menacingly in her direction.

"You just take yourself off, now," he said. "Don't want your kind hanging around. Never get so much as a single coin from you nutters, do I? You just move along and make room for paying customers."

Nikki hitched up her Seeker's robe and disappeared back into the crowd. The last thing she wanted was to cause a scene and have the palace guards show up to see what the commotion was. She had spotted some of the guards on the outskirts of the pasture, quietly watching the crowd. She was surprised that they hadn't been searching the tournament looking for Gwen. Their lack of action made her nervous. Did Rufius have other, less conspicuous people out looking? The palace guards, with their shiny, clunking armor, were easy to spot and easy to avoid. But if Rufius had searchers dressed as ordinary citizens of Kingston that made things a lot more difficult. That smiling lady carrying a tray of pastries could be one of his searchers, or that man drinking a tankard of ale with such gusto that half of it was spilling down his tunic. Nikki raised an eyebrow as the man suddenly dropped his tankard and fell face first into the grass. Okay, maybe not him, she thought.

She weaved carefully through the crowd, trying to stay as inconspicuous as possible. She passed by the long lines at the brewers tents without giving the customers a second glance. It was unlikely that Gwen would stop to drink a tankard of ale while trying to flee from Rufius and his guards. She noticed that the crowd was starting to thin out. People were leaving the tent area and heading to the trampled grass where the wrestling and sword fighting was taking place. A burst of trumpet calls sounded and banners with pictures of swords and arrows were raised. It looked like some sort of competition was about to begin.

Nikki ducked under a canvas awning to get out of the flow of foot traffic. Under the shade of the awning was a stall selling potted plants of all sorts – parsley, basil, thyme, petunias, tomatoes, zucchini, string beans, marigolds, and lots of other plants she didn't recognize.

"Gotta rush, dearie," said a customer, handing a coin to the stall's owner. "The tourney's about to begin. I put a pile o'coin on Kincaid's son to take the medal in the broadsword. He's a big, strapping lad and swings that sword around like an angry bear. If he doesn't trip over his own feet he should do well." She hurried away with a potted begonia under her arm.

"Not going to the tournament?" asked a quiet voice.

Nikki jumped. The other customers had left and the owner of the stall was looking at her. The woman was about fifty, Nikki judged, with long brown hair turning gray, and kind brown eyes. She wore a long woolen dress splotched with dirt from her potted plants and her fingernails were blackened with soil.

Nikki's first instinct was to dart away. If she spoke the woman would probably notice that she wasn't a real Seeker. She considered trying to fake a Seeker mumble, but the woman was looking at her so kindly that Nikki found herself smiling under her mask. "I don't find wrestling or sword-fighting all that interesting," she said.

The woman smiled, the laugh lines around her eyes crinkling. "Nor do I. All that bashing and grunting. Quite uncivilized." She held out a ripe peach. "Have one. No charge. The trees in my orchard produced so many this year that they're rotting on the branches."

Nikki took the plump, fuzzy fruit. "Thanks. That's very nice of you." She raised her face mask up just enough to slip the peach under it and took a bite. "Mmm. Wonderful." As she chewed she noticed that the woman was petting something in her hand. It was a tiny, pure-white mouse, no longer than one of the woman's fingers. As she watched it ran up the woman's arm and perched on top of her head.

The woman laughed and plucked the mouse off of her head. "This is Rosie. I raised her from a pup, when she was no bigger than my fingernail. Rosie is a nickname, of course. Her full name is Rosamund, and her title is the Rose of Knowledge."

Rosie let out a squeak, as if acknowledging that it was obvious a mouse of her distinction would have a title.

Nikki laughed. "Can I hold her?"

The woman nodded and gently placed Rosie in Nikki's palm.

Nikki stroked the mouse's soft fur. Rosie peered up at her with sharp black eyes and her tiny nose twitched, as if she'd seen through Nikki's Seeker mask and knew she was an imposter. Nikki felt Cation squirm inside her rucksack and she quickly handed the mouse back to the woman.

"I'm Linnea, by the way," said the woman.

"Oh, like the Linnaean System," said Nikki without thinking.

The woman's eyebrows rose in surprise. "The what?"

Nikki mentally smacked herself on the head. Seekers from the Realm of Reason didn't go around making remarks about a system of classifying species. Especially since the Linnaean System hadn't been invented in the Realm. It had been invented in her own world by a Swedish botanist called Carl Linnaeus. The system organized all plants and animals into a hierarchy of kingdom, class, order, genus, and species. Linnaeus had developed his system nearly three hundred years ago and the modern system had added family and phylum to it, though she could never remember where they went. Was it phylum, kingdom, class? Or kingdom, phylum, class? She'd failed that exact question about the Linnaean System on her Biology mid-term. "Um, nothing," mumbled Nikki. "It's not important."

The woman was still looking at her curiously. She pointed at Nikki's hands. "You don't wear gloves," she said. "Kind of unusual, isn't it? All the Seekers I've ever seen have worn long gloves, all the way up to their elbows. They're terrified of any sunlight hitting their skin."

"Um . . ." said Nikki, pulling her hands inside the long sleeves of her robe. As she tried to think up some excuse for her bare hands she suddenly noticed that Linnea was looking past her with a tense expression on her face. Nikki turned and found herself face to face with Rufius.

He was dressed in his usual spotless black tunic. This one had silver filigree around the neckline and along the hem. His sandals were so clean that he could have been walking through a palace rather than a muddy cow pasture. His black eyes slid over Nikki's mask, robe, and cloak.

Nikki stood still as stone. A bead of sweat trickled down her neck. In the rucksack on her back she could feel Cation squirming. Did

Seekers have pets? If a meow came from under her cloak would it be a dead giveaway that she was an impostor?

Linnea's voice interrupted Nikki's panicked thoughts. "She's just a Seeker, my lord. She wanted some fruit to take back to the other members of her order." She gestured impatiently at Nikki. "In the back, girl. Inside the tent. I set aside a basket of apples for you. You can pay me later."

Nikki felt Rufius watching her as she passed through the rows of potted plants and into the cool darkness of the heavy canvas tent. Baskets and boxes piled high with peaches, apples, and pears filled the tent. The air was heavy with the scent of ripe fruit and potting soil. In the back of the tent loomed a row of potted fruit trees. Nikki ducked behind these and peered out from between the branches. Linnea was pointing off into the distance toward the sword-fighting area of the pasture. Rufius glanced briefly in the direction she was pointing, then turned back and stared at the tent.

"He's going to come in!" whispered a voice right behind Nikki.

Nikki gasped and nearly fell face-first into the potted trees.

"Shhh! He'll hear you!"

It was Gwendolyn, hiding behind a potted blueberry bush. Her face was smudged with soot, her grey dress had a large burn mark on the skirt, and one of her hands was wrapped in a bloody bandage.

Nikki crawled behind the blueberry bush and gave Gwen a quick hug. "It's so good to see you again. Are you hurt?" she whispered.

Gwendolyn didn't answer. She was staring intently out at Rufius.

Linnea was now standing in front of him, blocking the way into the tent. Rosie the mouse was perched on her head, squeaking furiously at Rufius.

Nikki gasped. Rufius had raised his hand, and it looked for a moment like he was going to hit Linnea. But instead he put his fingers to his lips and gave a piercing whistle. Somewhere out in the pasture a clanking sound began, drawing closer and closer to the tent.

"Guards!" whispered Gwendolyn. "Come on!" She grabbed Nikki's sleeve and pulled her toward the back of the tent. The canvas sides of the tent were held down by wooden spikes driven into the ground. Gwendolyn snatched up a trowel from a box of gardening tools and attacked the dirt around a spike. When the spike was loose she grabbed it and pulled. A six-inch-high gap appeared, just tall enough for them to squirm under. Gwendolyn was through in a flash, but the gap wasn't high enough for both Nikki and her rucksack. She wriggled in frustration, trapped by her heavy Seeker robes. Cation yowled from inside the rucksack.

"Come on!" hissed Gwendolyn, pulling on Nikki's shoulders.

"Guards! In here!" shouted a voice only a few feet away. Rufius was right behind them, inside the tent.

Nikki gave one last desperate squirm and Gwendolyn yanked with all her might. Darkness suddenly descended on them. The tent had collapsed. Behind her she heard Rufius swearing. Nikki crawled in the opposite direction, pushing through the heavy canvas folds of the collapsed tent. She felt a tug on her arm and Gwendolyn pulled her out onto the grass behind the tent.

Nikki ripped off her face mask and squirmed out of her heavy Seeker cloak and robe. Underneath she had on her jeans and the blue silk tunic which Kira had given her back at the Prince's house. Much better. Now she could run. The only question was which way. She glanced quickly over her shoulder. The lump which was Rufius was still wrestling with the collapsed tent. She could hear the palace guards approaching but none were in sight yet.

"Now what?" she whispered to Gwen. "I'm supposed to meet Athena, Fuzz, and Curio in that corn field." She pointed back over her shoulder. "They're all searching for you too."

Gwen shook her head. "We don't want to lead Rufius and his guards straight to them. Follow me. I know a place we can hide." She dashed off toward a clump of trees on the edge of the fairground.

Nikki bit her lip and turned to look back at the distant stalks of the corn field. She didn't want to get separated from Fuzz and Athena again, but the sounds of rattling armor were getting closer and closer. She had no choice. She ran after Gwen.

Chapter Two

The Rose of Knowledge

NIKKI STRETCHED OUT full length on the lawn, wriggling her bare feet in delight. She and Gwen had spent hours running through the fields and forests around Kingston, trying to avoid capture by fording streams, climbing hills, getting scratched by brambles and the thorns of blackberry bushes, swimming across a lake, and hiding from every passerby. It was sheer heaven to lay still and rest. She closed her eyes as a cool breeze wafted the smell of ripening peaches over her. She hadn't explored all of it yet, but the garden she was in was quickly becoming her favorite place in the Realm of Reason.

It belonged to Linnea, the plant-lady who'd been hiding Gwen in her tent at the tournament. The garden was tucked away in a deep valley miles from Kingston. At the edge of the lawn was Linnea's thatched-roof cottage, its stone walls covered with purple morning-glory vines. The cottage was surrounded by a rose garden, a vegetable garden and an apple orchard. According to Gwen they would be spending several days here while they tried to track down Athena, Fuzz, and Curio. That was fine with Nikki. She needed a bit of a vacation from her adventures. It had been a whirlwind of activity ever since she stepped through that old boiler in the janitor's closet back home. She just hoped that Linnea was right about this place being impossible for Rufius and his guards to find. She wasn't sure exactly what Rufius would do if he caught her and Gwen, but she had a feeling that a dungeon was involved and she'd seen enough of the one in Castle Cogent to last a lifetime. Rats, cockroaches and the smell of raw sewage were not her favorite things.

"These strange shoes are falling apart. We'll have to see about getting you some new ones."

Nikki opened one eye. Gwen was holding up one of her Nikes. The rubber sole had almost completely detached from the uppers. Running all over the countryside had torn them up beyond repair.

Gwen prodded the sole with her finger. "What is this material?" she asked.

"Rubber," said Nikki. "Artificial rubber, anyway."

Gwen folded and twisted the sole. "It's so malleable. We don't have anything like it here in the Realm. How is it made?"

"Originally it came from rubber trees," said Nikki. "From the sap of the rubber tree. They used to carve a shallow trough into the bark of the tree. The sap would run down the trough and collect in a bucket. But I don't think my shoes are made of real rubber. My land produces an artificial kind of rubber." She closed her eyes again and hoped that Gwen was going to drop the subject. Trying to explain about artificial rubber was going to involve details about her world she wasn't sure she wanted to get into. She'd never really discussed her world with Gwen. Gwen knew she was a foreigner, but she didn't know from where. Athena and Fuzz had warned her not to let people know that she wasn't from the Realm of Reason. She'd tried to follow their advice, but it was hard with people she liked, like Gwen, Curio, and Kira. It was natural to want to share stuff about your life with friends, and Gwen was the closest thing to a friend she had in the Realm. She was fond of Athena and Fuzz, but they were a lot older than she was, and they had important things to do. Like trying to prevent Rufius and Maleficious from taking over the Realm.

As far as she knew, Athena, Fuzz, and the King were the only people in the Realm who knew where she came from. She thought back to her first meeting with Gwen at Gwen's ancestral home, Muddled Manor. She'd been so thrilled to meet someone who loved chemistry as much as she did that she'd told Gwen a lot about her high school's chemistry lab and the technical equipment it had. Back then she'd just arrived in the Realm and hadn't had time to understand just how backward the Realm was in terms of scientific discoveries. And it was only after she'd met greedy and ruthless people in the Realm, people like Rufius, Fortuna, and Avaricious, people who might use technology to harm others, that she realized she needed to be careful about what she said.

"This artificial rubber . . ." began Gwen.

"There you two are."

Nikki tilted her head back and squinted up at the sloping lawn. Linnea was coming toward them with Rosie the mouse riding proudly on top of her head like a tiny white figurehead on a sailing ship. Nikki sat up and waved.

"Sorry I took so long to get here," said Linnea, sitting down on the grass beside them. "I thought it best to take as many back roads as possible after I left the tournament, to be sure I wasn't followed." She folded back a red-and-white checked cloth which covered the basket she'd been carrying. A delicious smell of just-baked bread wafted up from it. "I'm sure you two are ravenous. I've got a stew simmering on the stove, but this should tide you over until it's ready." She pried the top off a jar of jam and spread it on a thick slice of warm bread. "Blueberry," she said, handing the bread to Nikki. "I had a spectacular crop this year. We're practically drowning in blueberries here. I tried out a new method of fertilization and it worked like a charm." She handed Gwen a slice of bread and bit into one herself. Rosie scampered down from her head and nibbled at the crumbs Linnea held in her palm.

Out of the corner of her eye Nikki noticed that her rucksack, which she'd dropped on the lawn beside her, was writhing like a python. She snatched up Cation just in time, grabbing the kitten by the scruff of the neck as she shot out of the rucksack and launched herself at Rosie.

Rosie squeaked in terror and dived into Linnea's sleeve. Linnea raised her arm protectively, cupping her elbow where Rosie was huddled inside her sleeve in a trembling lump. "I wasn't aware you had a cat," she said, eyeing Cation with a hint of unfriendliness. "As a rule I don't allow them here. Rosie is not my only pet. I also have a chipmunk called Nutter and a parrot called Samson. Your kitten could seriously injure them. Though old Samson would put up a good fight. He's got quite a vicious bite when he's cranky, which is most of the time."

"I think I can manage it so that Nikki's kitten isn't a problem," said Gwen. She tore a long skinny strip off the hem of her dress and quickly fashioned a little harness. She slipped it over Cation's head and around her chest, tightening it just enough so that the kitten couldn't squirm out of it. "There," she said. "As long as she's on her leash she shouldn't be a danger to your animals."

Cation growled and blinked up at Gwen with a petulant expression, as if to say she'd be a danger to anything she liked, but eventually she quieted down and curled up in Nikki's lap. She let Nikki feed her pieces of jam-covered bread while she kept a sharp eye on Linnea's elbow and hissed softly.

"Really wonderful jam," said Gwen, wiping her mouth.

Linnea nodded. "Yes, as I said, we had bushels of blueberries this year. I've sold hundreds of jars of jam at the market in Kingston. It was dried cow's dung which produced such a large crop. I put it around the roots of the blueberry bushes and they grew much faster than usual. I believe there is something in the dung which causes plants to grow."

"Nitrogen," said Nikki, licking her jam-covered fingers. "It increases plant size and the amount of fruit a bush will produce." She was now mentally checking practically everything she said while in the Realm of Reason, but she didn't see how any harm could come from mentioning nitrogen to Linnea and Gwen. It wasn't a harmful element like uranium or a valuable one like gold. Avaricious and Fortuna had tried to force her to produce gold from lead, but she seriously doubted that there was anyone in Kingston who was desperate to produce more cow manure. "It's one of the elements in the Periodic Table, a type of classification system we've developed in my land which describes the properties of metals, metalloids, the Noble Gases, and other elements. Nitrogen is element number seven in the table, and cow manure contains a lot of it. Gardeners and farmers in my land use manure to help plants grow. We call it fertilizer."

Linnea was looking at Nikki in such surprise that Gwen laughed. "You'll have to excuse Nikki," she said. "She suffers from the same disease I do: obsession with alchemy."

"Chemistry," said Nikki. "We call it chemistry in my land."

Gwen nodded. "Chemistry. Yes, you told me that back in my basement laboratory in Muddled Manor." She sighed. "I sometimes wish I was back there. Mother is a pain, but I do miss my lovely laboratory. All my distillation glassware that took me years to collect. I hope mother hasn't thrown it all out. I was quite surprised when I left home and went to work in Avaricious's shop in Deceptionville. I had expected such a large business to have an extensive laboratory, but mine was much better than Avaricious's."

Linnea chuckled. "Good old Avaricious. Such a greedy lump of lard, strutting around Deceptionville, obsessed with getting rich. I suppose I shouldn't laugh. He treats his workers terribly. Like slaves. Though I have to admit I do love to browse in his shop. He has such a wonderful collection of dried herbs from all over the Realm and even some from the Southern Isles."

"That's how Linnea and I know each other," said Gwen to Nikki. "I was working in Avaricious's shop one day, distilling an essence of lavender, when Linnea came in and asked for nightshade root. One of the other workers heard her and ran out of the shop to find a Rounder. Linnea nearly got arrested. I had to hustle her out the back door."

"Why?" asked Nikki.

"Nightshade's a deadly poison," said Linnea. "The Rounders keep track of who buys it, probably so someone doesn't use it to poison the Deceptionville town council, not that that would be a very great loss. They're a bunch of bribe-taking moochers. Anyway, nightshade is very difficult to grow, so I have to buy it. I make a special trip to Deceptionville every year just for it. Avaricious's shop is one of the only places in the Realm which has it. I bought a few seeds of it last year from a trader from the Southern Isles, but I wasn't able to cultivate the plant. The seeds won't sprout in this climate."

"But if it's poisonous why would you want it?" asked Nikki.

"It causes numbness and sleepiness in small doses," said Linnea. "I often get local farmers calling on me when one of their children has broken an arm or leg. I have some skill in setting broken bones. In addition to my work with plants I have long studied the bones of small animals such as the mice and foxes which have died in my fields. Their skeletal structures are fascinating. Each type of animal has a different skeleton, yet they all share basic components such as a backbone. From studying the skeletons I learned how the different bones joined together and how to splint them when they were broken. I started helping lame dogs, but soon found that the same type of setting and splinting would work on humans. I give the injured animal or person a small dose of nightshade root steeped in water. They fall into a deep sleep and I am able to set their broken bone without causing them pain. It works much better than the old practice of giving them alcohol. Drunk people can still feel pain. But I have to be very careful with the dosage when I use nightshade. Give too much and you can easily kill your patient. I had Dolor, the local Toothpuller, come around last month asking me for some, but I had to refuse. He's not the most reliable person. When he's wielding his pliers on someone's tooth he's usually as drunk as his patient. You should see the bloody mess he makes of people's mouths. He definitely isn't capable of carefully measuring a dose of nightshade."

"Instead of getting his patients drunk he could try numbing the nerve of the tooth," said Nikki, whose skin was crawling at the thought of someone with pliers yanking out one of her teeth. She'd always hated going to the dentist, but at that moment she was intensely grateful for modern dentistry and its needles full of Novocain.

"What is a nerve?" asked Linnea.

"It's a kind of pathway in the body which transmits pain," replied Nikki. Her mind was spinning with worry again about what to say next. She was having the same kind of debate with herself that she'd had back in the Prince's old laboratory in the Southern Castle. How much modern knowledge should she introduce to the Realm of Reason? Obviously anything which could be used to create weapons was out of the question, but what about medical knowledge which might help ease suffering? Not that medicine was a subject she knew much about. Chemistry was more her thing. But her AP Biology class had included some basic human anatomy. When they'd discussed nerve endings and various ways to ease pain her teacher had mentioned that an extract from the leaves of the coca tree was chemically similar to Novocain. It had been used by dentists back in the nineteenth century to help with tooth pain. She wondered if the Realm of Reason had something similar to a coca tree.

"You mentioned that you bought some nightshade seeds from a trader from the Southern Isles," said Nikki. "Did you buy any other plants from him?"

Linnea nodded. "I always buy a little of whatever he has, whether I need it or not. It's a long journey from the Southern Isles and he doesn't come around here very often."

"These Southern Isles," said Nikki, "are they tropical?"

Linnea frowned. "Tropical? I'm not familiar with the word."

"It means a place which is hot and rainy, with lots of jungles. Lots of vines and snakes and trees which are different from the pines and oaks you have here."

"Yes, that sounds like the Southern Isles," said Linnea. "I've never been there myself, but I've heard sailors at the port in Kingston say that the air in the Southern Isles is so full of water that a person can hardly breathe, and that there are vines hanging from the trees as thick as your arm."

Nikki nodded. She was going to try to introduce a new painkilling technique to the Realm of Reason. It just seemed like the right thing to do. She couldn't get the horrible picture of the local tooth-puller out of her mind. She might have an opportunity to save people a lot of pain and it seemed wrong not to try. "Let's go take a look at the plants you've collected from the Southern Isles," she said.

Linnea looked a little surprised, but she shrugged good-naturedly and gathered up her basket, cradling her elbow where the lump which was Rosie still trembled.

Nikki racked her brain as she scooped up Cation and followed Gwen and Linnea across the lawn toward Linnea's cottage. She was trying to remember that day back in her biology class when her teacher had talked about nerve pain and dentistry. What was the guy's name? Halsted? That sounded right. William Halsted. Sometime in the 1880's he'd used coca extract as a local anesthetic during a dental procedure. He'd used a four percent solution of coca in alcohol, injected with a hypodermic needle into the patient's gum near the tooth he was going to pull. She knew her extract would be crude, as she didn't have access to sophisticated lab equipment, but she was pretty sure she could produce a workable painkiller. If it worked it would be much safer than the nightshade Linnea used. Since Linnea's patients swallowed the nightshade it affected their whole body. The coca-leaf extract she hoped to produce would be injected, affecting only one nerve next to one tooth. The patient would never be unconscious the way they were with nightshade, so they would never be in danger of having their heart or breathing stop. A pang of doubt suddenly stopped her in her tracks. Coca leaves could be addictive. She didn't want to be responsible for creating drug addicts in the Realm of Reason. She sighed. She wished her mother was there to advise her.

"Nikki? Are you all right?" asked Gwen.

Nikki looked up, surprised to find herself standing in the doorway of Linnea's cottage. She gave Gwen a reassuring smile. "Sure. I'm fine. Just thinking over some stuff." She crossed the threshold into the main room of the cottage. It was a sturdy, comforting room with thick stone walls and a huge fireplace blackened with soot.

Linnea set her basket down on the heavy oak dining table in the middle of the room. A tiny striped chipmunk suddenly darted into the room and scampered across the dining table. It dived headfirst into the basket. The red and white checked cloth covering the basket twitched furiously and the chipmunk reappeared dragging a piece of bread.

"This is Nutter," said Linnea, stroking the chipmunk's striped back as it ferociously devoured the bread, scattering crumbs across the tabletop.

"It looks like he hasn't eaten in a week," laughed Gwen.

"Nutter always eats as if he's starving," said Linnea. "If he doesn't eat his food quickly Samson swoops in and snatches it right from under his nose."

"Who's Samson?" asked Nikki.

Linnea pointed over their heads at a large parrot with gorgeous red and blue feathers who had flown in through the open doorway.

The parrot let out an ear-piercing squawk at the sight of Nutter and his piece of bread. He went into a dive, claws outstretched, and snatched up both the chipmunk and the piece of bread. He circled twice around the room and then unceremoniously dropped Nutter down the mouth of a tall stone vase near the front door. Samson gracefully landed on the mantelpiece and balanced on one claw while he lifted the bread to his beak with the other. Unlike the unfortunate Nutter he nibbled with lazy delicacy, as if well aware that no one would dare snatch food from out of his sharp beak.

Linnea reached an arm into the stone vase and retrieved the chipmunk, who ran up her arm and perched on her shoulder. Rosie the mouse wriggled out of Linnea's sleeve and perched on her other shoulder.

Gwen laughed. "You've got quite a menagerie."

"Oh, these are just the house pets," said Linnea. "I've also got a goat, a coop full of chickens, two cows and a dog we named Tripod, because she has only three legs. I've loved animals since I was a child. I used to keep pet mice in my room, which my mother hated. She was always setting out traps for them, but I used to take the cheese out of the traps and feed it to the mice until they were tame." She plucked the chipmunk off her shoulder and put it back into the bread basket. "Nutter joined the household when I rescued him from a hawk, and I purchased Samson from a trader from the Southern Isles. The same trader I get my herbs from, actually. Anyway, enough about my pets. You wanted to see my herb collection. It's in the pantry. This way."

Nikki and Gwen followed her down the hall into a small room next to the kitchen. A whiff of sulfur wafted through the air as Linnea scratched a match against the stone wall and lit a candle to light the windowless room. "I have quite a collection, as you can see," she said, sweeping her hand around the room. It was lined floor to ceiling with shelves piled high with straw baskets and clay pots. "I've been collecting herbs, and seeds since I was a child. I've lost count, but I must have over a thousand different kinds."

"What beautiful carnations," said Gwen, pointing to a glass vase filled with light-green carnations glowing in the candlelight. "I've never seen them that color before."

Linnea plucked one from the vase and twirled it in her fingers. "The color is artificial. I start with white carnations and add spinach leaves to the water in the vase. I'm studying how water is transported through the stem of a plant up to its leaves and flowers."

"Capillary action," said Nikki.

"Pardon?" said Linnea.

"It's called capillary action," said Nikki. "The water flows from the roots of the plant up through its xylem tissue, which is kind of like a tube or vein in the stem of the plant, and then up to the leaves and flowers. When the sun shines on the leaves of a plant water evaporates from the leaves, causing depressurization at the top of the plant. When there's lower pressure at the top and higher pressure at the bottom it helps push the water upwards. Adhesion is involved too. We covered it in school, but I don't remember the details. Something about adhesion of water molecules to the xylem tissue in the stem also helps the water rise."

Linnea stared at her, mouth open.

Gwen laughed. "Nikki is quite educated, as you can see," she said. "I've been working away at my experiments in my mother's basement at Muddled Manor for years, and I foolishly thought I knew more than anyone in the Realm about the properties of metals and other elements. But then I met Nikki."

Nikki was glad the room was dark. She could feel her face turning red. "I just had good teachers," she said. "And my mother is an expert in her field. She performs experiments similar to Gwen's. She's taught me a lot." She knelt down and sniffed at some dried pods containing tiny black seeds. "So, are these from the Southern Isles?" she asked, trying to change the subject.

Linnea was still staring at her, but she eventually shook her head and led them over to a row of shelves against the far wall. "This is my Southern Isles collection."

Nikki peered into the pots and baskets filled with seeds and dried plants. She'd seen coca leaves in person once. A girl who'd emigrated from Peru had brought some of the leaves into her biology class. The girl had told the class that Peruvians living high up in the Andes Mountains chewed the coca leaves as a remedy for altitude sickness. She'd passed the leaves around the class and Nikki had tried one. The leaf had an unpleasant, bitter taste and had left her mouth feeling numb. As near as she could remember the leaf had been small, oblong, and dark green . . . Nikki picked a leaf out of a clay pot and sniffed it. No, the smell was too sweet. She nibbled on one from a reed basket. No, the taste was wrong. She sniffed another candidate. Maybe. She broke off a tiny piece and cautiously chewed it. Yes, this might be it. The same bitter taste, the same mild numbness on her tongue.

"Can I take a few of these?" she asked.

"Certainly, if you wish," said Linnea. "They're just gathering dust. I've never figured out a use for them. The trader I bought them from said the islanders boil them to make a tea. I tried that but it tasted terrible."

"In my land we don't use this for tea," said Nikki. "We make a kind of painkiller from it."

Linnea's eyes widened. "Really? How interesting. Can you show me how to make it? I'm always looking for better ways to help the local villagers with their health problems. And they would be thrilled with anything which makes the Toothpuller's visits less painful."

Nikki nodded. "I was thinking exactly the same thing. I'm not sure I can do it, but if my idea works it will be much better than giving your patients alcohol or nightshade."

Chapter Three

The Toothpuller

NIKKI BLEW OUT the flame burning in an oil lamp. A small clay pot rested on an iron trestle above the lamp, its bottom warmed by the flame. A wisp of steam floated above the liquid in the pot. Nikki sniffed it. The concentrated liquid still had tiny pieces of leaves floating in it, but she was pretty sure it was at least a four percent solution of coca in alcohol. It might even be a bit stronger. The only way to be sure was to test it. And that presented its own problems, especially the problem of the delivery system. An injection was the best way to get her solution close to a nerve, but the Realm was unlikely to have hypodermic needles. Just rubbing it on a patient's gums or having them swish it in their mouth wasn't going to be enough. She was just pouring the solution into a small glass jar and sealing the jar with a cork when she heard what sounded like imp voices out in the main room of the house. She set the jar on a shelf and rushed out of the pantry.

"Miss! You are all right! We were so worried!" Athena ran up to Nikki and grabbed her hand, squeezing it tightly. The imp had shed her bulky Seeker robes and was once again in her prim grey dress, which was unwrinkled and spotless despite her journey.

Nikki bent down and gave the imp a hug. "I'm fine. So is Gwen."

Fuzz was sitting on a chair next to the dining table, his short legs swinging a foot off the ground. He gave her a cheeky wink. He had also disposed of his robes and was back in his usual trousers, shirt and embroidered vest, none of which was spotless and all of which smelled of ale. "Of course you're fine. I told Miss Worrywart to stop her fussing, but she was sure you were all dead in a ditch somewhere or locked away in the deepest dungeon of the Southern Castle. A place, by the way, which I happen to have a personal acquaintance with. I'm afraid I can't recommend the accommodations. The beds are flea-covered piles of hay and the rats are way too friendly. I don't mind rats when they know their place, but their place is not inside my pant leg."

"Hello, Miss" mumbled Curio through a mouthful of jam-smeared bread. He was sitting on a faded armchair near the fireplace, his thin legs crossed beneath him. He pointed to the brown linen trousers he was wearing. "Look, Miss. Mr. Fuzz got me brand new clothes at the tournament! Never had new clothes before. They make me feel quite fancy. And I can tell they're good quality, cause of how much they itch."

"How did you find us?" asked Nikki. "This place seems pretty out of the way."

"The imp code," said Fuzz, as if that explained everything.

"We imps have certain ways of communicating with each other over long distances," said Athena in response to Nikki's confused expression. "We call it the imp code, but that is just the language we use. The language can be communicated in many different forms. Sometimes we use smoke signals, sometimes flashes of light bounced off small mirrors, sometimes drum beats, sometimes brightly colored flags. Even if a big person were to notice the smoke puffs or the flashes of light they wouldn't be able to understand what we were saying, as they don't know the imp code. The language."

Nikki nodded. "We have something similar in my land called Morse Code. It's a series of dots and dashes, short sounds and long sounds, which represent letters. But, if you sent an imp code signal, who received it? From what I've heard, imps are rare in this part of the Realm. They're being driven out by Rufius."

"Tarn," said Fuzz, ignoring Athena as she winced at the name. "Okay, maybe he's not the nicest person you'll ever meet, not exactly an imp of the highest quality. He's a bit of a lowbrow good-for-nothing."

Athena gave him a meaningful look.

Fuzz waived an impatient hand at her. "Yeah, I know. Lots of people have said the same thing about me. And maybe they have a point. But despite our shortcomings Tarn and I both try to help out our fellow imps when we can. We waited for you in the corn field for a long time, but the palace guards started searching the field. It was only a matter of time until they found us, so we had to leave. We made for the oak woods just north of the tournament and lit a fire. Athena sent a smoke message toward Kingston harbor. Tarn picked it up and replied back. We told him we'd lost you and he set the imp network in motion. The network isn't all imps. Quite a few big people are willing to help us, despite the dangers. People like Linnea, for instance."

"Yes, there are more of us around here who are sympathetic to the imps than you might think," said Linnea, swooping into the room, a pile of plates in one hand and a basket of bread in the other. She and her cook quickly set the table. The cook was a grumpy man built like a bulldog who scowled at everyone as if daring them to eat anything he'd made. The gardeners and farmhands who worked Linnea's lands came in and they were all about to sit down and tuck into a huge pot of stew and piles of fresh-baked bread with just-churned butter when a piercing scream came from outside the front door.

They all jumped up from the table. The front door banged open and a small boy rushed in, screaming at the top of his lungs. He ran to

Linnea and hid behind her, clutching desperately at her skirt.

"Don't let him near me, Miss," shrieked the boy. "He'll tear my whole head off with those pinchers of his. I swear he will."

"I'm not going ta tear your head off, you stupid brat. Just yer teeth."

Nikki had to bite back a scream herself when the man who had spoken stepped through the doorway. He looked like a dead person who had thrown back the lid of his coffin and walked into his own funeral. He was well over six feet tall, with skin the color of spoiled milk. His skull-like head held teeth so black they looked like pieces of coal. In one hand he held a pair of pliers. Their tip was coated with something that looked suspiciously like blood.

"Hello Dolor," said Linnea calmly. "I see you're still plying your trade."

Dolor grinned wickedly, the stench of alcohol streaming from his rotting teeth. "Aye, and I'll keep doing it long as it pays. Which it does." He pointed his bloody pliers at the boy shivering behind Linnea. "This one's parents are paying me two gold coins, real gold, mind you, to yank out 'is front teeth. And no amount of 'is screeching is goin ta keep me from my pay."

Linnea frowned and knelt down in front of the little boy, gently taking his jaw in her hand. "Open your mouth, sweetheart. Let me take a quick look."

Tears sprouted from the boy's eyes, but he nodded and slowly opened his mouth.

Nikki gasped and put a hand over her mouth. The smell was so strong she thought for a moment she was going to vomit. I was a smell she recognized. One she would never forget. When she was six she'd had an abscessed tooth. It had become infected and her mother had taken her to the dentist to have it pulled out. She'd screamed so much that the dentist had to put her under. When she'd woken up there was a bloody hole in her mouth that she kept poking her tongue into. The dentist had given her antibiotics for the infection, but she'd never forgotten the smell.

"Oh, honey," said Linnea softly. "I'm so sorry, but those two front teeth of yours definitely need to come out. They're both rotten."

"But, but," sobbed the little boy, "they'll fall out by themselves. I know they will. All the kids in my village have their teeth fall out."

Linnea nodded. "You're right, they're baby teeth, but I'm afraid we can't wait for yours to fall out naturally. If we don't pull them out right now you'll get very sick. You might even die."

Dolor advanced on the little boy, snapping his bloody pliers. "Time for me ta earn me pay." He gestured at the cook. "Plop 'im in that chair by the fire and hold 'im down. Hold 'im down good, specially his legs. Yesterday one of the little brats I was workin' on kicked me right in me privates."

The cook stepped toward the little boy, but Nikki blocked his way. "Wait," she said. "You can't just yank out his teeth. The pain will be terrible."

Dolor shrugged. "Pain's part of life. And it's specially part of tooth-pullin'." He grinned and snapped his pliers at the boy.

"Nikki's right," said Linnea. "We can at least ease his suffering before you start yanking. I'll get my nightshade mixture."

Linnea snatched a candle from the mantelpiece and hurried out of the room. Nikki followed.

"I don't have much nightshade left," said Linnea as she rushed into the pantry and snatched up a tiny glass bottle with a wax stopper. "But it should be enough to put the child under. It won't take much. He's very small. Normally I don't like to give nightshade to children that tiny. It overwhelms their system and can stop their breathing. But I can't just stand by while Dolor tortures the poor child."

Nikki put a hand on her arm. "I have a better idea. I hope" She retrieved the solution of coca leaves in alcohol she had distilled. "This is the painkiller I was talking about. We use it in my land to numb a tooth before pulling it. I believe it will ease the boy's pain without having to knock him unconscious with nightshade. It will be much safer."

Linnea took the bottle from her and held it up to the candlelight. A few bits of green leaves swirled in the cloudy liquid. She gave Nikki a doubtful look. "Are you sure about this? Will it really work as you say?"

"Yes," said Nikki with more confidence than she felt. "I just need a delivery system."

Linnea looked at her in confusion.

"A needle," said Nikki. "A very, very thin one. In my land we use what we call a hypodermic needle to inject the painkiller into the tooth, but you don't have those here so we'll have to use a regular needle. It won't work quite as well, and we'll probably have to jab the boy's gums multiple times unfortunately. That will hurt, but not as much as having his teeth yanked out by the roots without any painkiller at all."

Linnea looked at her thoughtfully. "We need to jab his tooth?"

Nikki nodded. "Down below the gum line. At the bottom of the tooth, where the root is."

Linnea handed Nikki the bottle of coca solution and reached up to the top shelf again. She took down a small wooden box and opened its lid. "Nightshade paste," she said. "It's my nightshade solution in concentrated form, with all the water evaporated. I mix it with a little beeswax to keep it soft. I use it when someone has a small cut or puncture wound. It numbs the skin for several hours, making the wound less painful. I was thinking, if we rub the boy's gums with this before you jab him with the needle it will make the jabs less painful. And since he won't be swallowing it there's not much danger that it will cause him to stop breathing."

"Yes, that's a very good idea," said Nikki, trying to smile at Linnea, though her hands trembled and her stomach jolted. It had never occurred to her that *she* would be the one doing the jabbing. She'd assumed that Linnea would be the one wielding the needle. Before she knew it Linnea had plucked a needle from a sewing kit in a corner of the pantry and was leading her back to the main room.

The little boy was huddled in the armchair in front of the fire, Curio's arm protectively circling his shoulders.

"Curio," said Nikki, "why don't you go and sit at the table. Have some stew."

Curio's normally cheerful face turned stormy. "I won't, Miss, begging your pardon. He's in awful pain, he is. I won't let anyone pull out his teeth just for sport." He put a finger in the gap where his own front tooth had fallen out. "My tooth fell out on its own. Don't see why his can't. And mine's growing back in, too." He tapped the stub of a new tooth which was poking through his gums.

Nikki crossed her arms and assumed what she hoped was a Mom-like expression. "Curio, you know very well that I'd never hurt anyone just for fun. We have to do this or he'll die. It's as simple as that. Now go to the table and eat your dinner."

Curio reluctantly slid off the chair and backed away a few feet.

Nikki didn't want him watching this, but she didn't have time to argue with him. Her hands were already starting to shake. If she waited any longer nerves would get the better of her and it would be impossible to do what needed to be done. She nodded at Linnea.

Linnea knelt down in front of the chair and gently opened the boy's mouth. She dipped her finger in the nightshade paste and rubbed it into the gums near the boy's two front teeth. The boy winced and hastily wiped away a tear, but he didn't resist.

"It works quickly," said Linnea, getting to her feet. "Go ahead."

Nikki nodded, her heart racing. She knelt in front of the chair and peered into the boy's mouth, her already churning stomach becoming even more upset from the smell. She pulled the stopper off her bottle of coca solution and dipped Linnea's needle in it. Hypodermic needles were hollow. When her dentist back home pushed the plunger the Novocain was forced through the hollow needle and into her gum. Since she didn't have a hypodermic needle her plan was to jab the gum and let the solution run down the outside of the needle. The amount of solution she could administer this way was small, so she'd need multiple jabs to thoroughly numb each tooth. With one shaking hand she gently pricked the gum just above the boy's front teeth.

Linnea laid a hand on Nikki's shoulder. "You'll need to jab harder, I'm afraid. You aren't doing the boy any favors by holding back."

Nikki nodded, a tear running down her cheek. This was one of the hardest things she'd ever had to do. She dipped the needle in the solution again and held the boy's chin with her other hand. This time she plunged the needle in until it wouldn't go in any farther. She watched as the liquid ran down the side of the needle and into the tiny hole she'd made.

After five more jabs Nikki stood up, her legs trembling. "I think that will do it."

Dolor grunted and advanced on the boy. "Bout time. Ain't got all day. Don't know why we're messing about with silly needles anyways. The boy's not a pincushion."

"Wait!" said Nikki. "The painkiller will take a few minutes to work. You can't pull his teeth just yet. And before you do I insist that you wash your pliers. They're so dirty you'll give the boy an infection."

Dolor glared at her, but Linnea nodded. "Quite right," she said. "Hand them over." She held out her palm.

Dolor's skull-like face darkened, but he finally handed over his pliers and retreated to the table, where he began eating stew straight out of the pot with his fingers.

Nikki followed Linnea into the kitchen. In one corner a small hole had been cut into the thick stone wall and a clay pipe jutted out. Water trickled from the pipe into a wooden barrel.

"The village stonecutter arranged this for me last year," said Linnea, sticking the bloody pliers under the running water. "It's quite handy. Before this was in place we used to have to carry buckets of water in from the well outside in the yard."

Nikki watched as blood dripped off the pliers into the barrel. "I hope you aren't going to drink this water," she said.

Linnea shook her head and pointed down at the floor. Another pipe ran out of the bottom of the barrel through a hole in the floor. "The drain is open. The dirty water runs out of the barrel and into a trench which runs the length of the house. Once the dirty water is flushed out I'll close the drain and we'll have clean drinking water again. Darius, that's our stonecutter, is quite an ingenious person. I'm thinking of introducing him to Gwendolyn. They both have the same kind of curious and innovative mind. I think they would get along very well, if you know what I mean." She winked playfully at Nikki. "Matchmaking isn't really my area of expertise, though, so I can't make any promises." She held the wet pliers up to the light from the open window. "That's as clean as this instrument of torture is going to get, I think. Best get this over with, for the boy's sake. The waiting can be the worst part, sometimes."

"Wait," said Nikki. "Do you have any alcohol?"

Linnea raised an eyebrow. "Alcohol? Aren't you a bit young to be drinking?"

"It's not for me," said Nikki. "It's for the pliers. To kill the germs."

"The what?" asked Linnea.

"The germs," said Nikki. "The bacteria. Even though the pliers look clean, I bet there's still millions of bacteria on it. Alcohol can kill them."

Linnea looked at her like she'd lost her mind. "There's nothing on the pliers. See?" She held them up to the light again.

"Bacteria are invisible to the naked eye. You'd need a microscope to see them." Nikki waved her hand impatiently as Linnea started to

33

say something. "I'll explain later. The boy's teeth should be numb by now. If we wait too long the painkiller will start to wear off." She glanced at the shelves lining the kitchen walls. "You must have some kind of alcohol here. Not ale or wine. Something clear, like vodka."

Linnea took a bottle down from a shelf. "I don't know what vodka is, but this is grain alcohol. We make it from barley."

Nikki nodded and took the bottle. "That should work." She un-corked the bottle and held the pliers over a basin sitting on the big wooden work table in the middle of the kitchen. She poured a good-sized helping of the alcohol over the pliers. "There, that should zap most of the germs." She handed the pliers back to Linnea. "If you don't mind, I think I'll wait here until Dolor has finished."

Linnea patted her on the shoulder. "Of course. You've done won-derfully well, my dear. I know it was difficult for you. Believe me, when I first started setting broken bones many years ago I was far more of a wreck than you are now. I would throw up, both before the procedure and after it." She hurried out of the kitchen with the pliers.

Nikki bent over the stone countertop which ran along one wall and rested her forehead on its cold surface. She held her hands over her ears, ready for the screams, but none came. After what seemed like hours but was probably only a few minutes she heard voices coming toward the kitchen.

Nikki lifted her head from the counter and saw the little boy with the rotten teeth standing in the doorway. There was blood dripping from his chin, but he was smiling. He rushed forward and took Nikki's hand.

"Look," he said, pointing at the gaping hole in his mouth where his two front teeth had been. "And it didn't even hurt. Miss Linnea says that you stopped the pain with your needles. It was like magic. Are you a wizard?"

Nikki laughed. "No, I'm not a wizard. I'm a scientist. At least, I want to be, when I'm older. My Mom's a scientist, and I want to be just like her."

"I want to be a scientist too," said the boy. "I don't know what a scientist is, but that's what I'm going to be when I grow up."

Nikki laughed again. "A scientist is someone who studies the natural world. Like Linnea. She studies plants and animal bones and farming. She's what my people would call a biologist. She's kind of like a bard of biology."

The boy nodded solemnly and wiped the blood off his chin. "That's what I want to be. A Bard of Biology. I'll ask Miss Linnea if I can 'prentice with her. I was 'sposed to 'prentice with a pig farmer in the next village, but being a Bard of Biology is much better than being a pig farmer."

"Prentice?" asked Nikki.

"Get trained up," said the boy. "You live with your master and get trained up so that when you're old enough you can take over and do the job yourself."

"Oh, right," said Nikki. "An apprenticeship. Yes, that's a very good idea."

"I'll go ask Miss Linnea right now," said the boy. He made Nikki a funny little bow and ran out of the kitchen.

Chapter Four

The Stonecutter

NIKKI YAWNED WIDELY as she sat at Linnea's dining table the next morning, slowly working her way through scrambled eggs and buttermilk biscuits. She'd gotten to bed very late. Linnea had left to return the little boy to his parents and then they'd all had to help her cook another stew, as no one wanted to eat the one that Dolor had put his grimy hands into. Even after she'd finally crawled under the covers Nikki had tossed and turned most of the night. Each time she fell asleep she had nightmares about dancing needles and bloody teeth. Today she wanted nothing more than another day lying in the sun on Linnea's lovely green lawn, staring up at the blue sky and not thinking anything or doing anything. Unfortunately, the whispers coming from the other end of the table did not bode well for this plan. Athena, Fuzz, Gwen and Linnea were huddled together, their heads bent in intense discussion.

A chair creaked as Athena pushed away from the table and came over to Nikki. "Miss, we have been planning."

Nikki winced and ate another forkful of eggs.

Athena put a hand on Nikki's arm and waited until Nikki looked at her. "Miss, as you know, the imps are having a very difficult time right now in the Realm. We have always had a few spots of trouble here and there because of our size and because there are so few of us.

36

But mostly we've been left in peace. But now, with Maleficious and Rufius targeting the imps things are becoming very bad. Linnea has told us that all of the imps have been driven out of the area around her farm. And that Rufius seems intent on driving all of the imps out of Kingston. We cannot let this happen. Kingston is a very important city in the Realm, second only to Deceptionville in power and wealth. If this hatred which Rufius is stirring up against the imps is allowed to fester it will affect the entire Realm. We must do something to stop it."

Nikki looked at her warily. "Like what, exactly?"

The imp looked up at her, a granite-hard expression on her face. "We are going back to Kingston. Fuzz and I are going to walk the streets of Kingston openly. No more hiding under Seeker robes. This is our Realm too. We will not skulk in the shadows like cowards."

Nikki dropped her fork. "Athena, are you nuts? You'll be arrested on sight. Rufius will throw you both into the dungeon of the Southern Castle."

"That is a possibility," said the imp calmly. "But the situation is not hopeless. We have allies in Kingston. Very powerful ones. The King and the Prince of Physics. It is true that the King has perhaps passed too much of his power and his duties to Maleficious, but he has always been a strong supporter of the imps. Whatever his faults, he will not stand by and see the imps mistreated."

Nikki's eyebrows rose. It seemed to her that the King had already done a lot of standing by. "Athena, are you sure . . ."

"It has been decided, Miss," said Athena firmly. "Miss Gwendolyn is going with us. We could not talk her out of it." The imp sighed. "I fear for her safety, but she is an adult and has the right to make up her own mind. You, however, are still a child. You are much too young to be involved in such a dangerous business. You will stay here with Linnea. The farmers and villagers in the area are very loyal to her. I do not think they will turn you in to Rufius and his guards. You should be safe here."

Nikki shoved back her chair and stood up. "Absolutely not. I'm coming with you. No arguments. If you try to make me stay here I'll just follow you. I'll be safer going with you than trying to follow you to Kingston on my own. Actually, I'll probably get lost. I'm not even sure which direction Kingston is. You don't want me wandering around the Realm all alone, do you?"

"Told you," called Fuzz from the other end of the table. "Might as well face it, Miss Prim. You never had any hope of convincing her to stay here." He hopped down from his chair as Athena glared at him. "Now, here's the plan," said Fuzz. "A rough outline, anyway. Linnea is going to introduce us to a stonecutter chap called Darius who lives here in the village. She says he has the tools and expertise to cut through anything. And the anything I want to cut through is the walls of the Southern Castle. Gwen has been telling us that while she was locked up in the castle she heard the guards talking about a band of imps who are being held prisoner in the deepest part of the dungeons. Seems the Knights of the Iron Fist managed to capture a few stragglers when they attacked our headquarters in the Trackless Forest. We're going to get them out."

"And to do that you're going to cut through the castle walls?" Nikki couldn't hide her skepticism. She'd seen the walls of the Southern Castle with her own eyes. They were solid stone at least ten-feet thick. "Wouldn't it be easier to just have Gwen blast them again?"

"I could," said Gwen, who was looking better after her day of rest at Linnea's. The bruise on her cheek had faded, she'd washed the soot out of her hair, and Linnea had given her a new dress of pale blue linen. "But it would make a very loud noise. Every palace guard within half a mile would rush to the spot. We'd all be captured for sure."

"Exactly," said Fuzz. "Now, I know the Southern Castle inside and out. I've been both a guest and a prisoner there. I preferred the former, but the latter was more useful. There's a network of water and sewage tunnels under the dungeons. They lead into various streams and reservoirs in Kingston, depending on whether it's water flowing in or poop flowing out."

Athena turned beet red. "You are *not* leading us through sewage tunnels. *You* may not mind the smell and the sticky mess, but the rest of us are not good-for-nothing, ale-swilling, beer-guzzling nincompoops who can't pass by a tavern without wallowing in the mud with the tavern-keeper's pigs."

"If your Highness is referring to the incident behind the Boar's Head Inn," said Fuzz, "it was only one pig and he was extremely clean. I needed a place to sleep off a few glasses of the best ale I've ever tasted and the pig was kind enough to let me share his straw. He made quite a well-behaved sleeping companion. He didn't even snore, unlike some people in this room who I could mention." He waggled his eyebrows at Athena.

"I do *not* . . ." said Athena. "I have *never* . . ."

Athena turned so red that Nikki was afraid she was going to have a seizure. She handed the imp a glass of water, which Athena grudgingly sipped, muttering in between swallows.

"As I was saying," continued Fuzz, "there are lots of tunnels under the castle. Whether the one we need is a water tunnel or a poop tunnel I can't remember. But I do remember several of the tunnels are right under the dungeons, and the dungeon floors aren't as thick as the walls. Linnea's stonecutter will only have to cut through about ten inches of stone, if he cuts up through the floor."

"But," said Nikki. "Even if you manage to get the imps out of the dungeon, where are they going to go? The palace guards and the Knights of the Iron Fist will just round them up again."

Fuzz shook his head. "Not if we play our cards right. Our best bet will be to lead the imps to the docks. Quarter them on Griff's ship. She's always been a friend to imps, she even has a few of us on her crew. And more importantly, she's related to the Prince of Physics.

That gives her a lot of pull in Kingston. The palace guards will think twice before trying to board her ship." Fuzz gulped down the last of the ale he'd been drinking for breakfast. "Rufius has been playing a dangerous game, bringing palace guards into the Prince's mansion and letting the Knights of the Iron Fist ride their horses through his rosebushes, but he hasn't quite declared full-scale war on the Prince. Not yet. Rufius knows that thousands of people in Kingston are still loyal to the King and to the Prince. What we're going to do is spread the news that an attack on the imps is an attack on the Prince. We'll use Griff's ship as our headquarters." He slammed his empty glass on the table. "Enough planning. Time to head out."

AFTER BREAKFAST LINNEA loaded them up with rucksacks and provisions for their trip back to Kingston. She pulled on a traveling cloak, tucked Rosie the mouse into her sleeve, and picked up a bag full of potions and dried herbs. "Okay, everybody ready?" she asked. "Rosie and I will walk with you as far as the village. I want to stop by the house of our little patient from last night to make sure he's not still bleeding. Sometimes Dolor's crude handiwork can make a person's gums bleed for a week or more. I make an anti-coagulant from dandelion greens which helps stop the bleeding."

"What's an anti-coggeley?" asked Curio, who was strapping on the tiny rucksack Linnea had packed for him.

"Anti-coagulant," corrected Linnea, straightening the twisted straps of Curio's rucksack. "It's something which can stop a person or an animal from bleeding. I first noticed that dandelion stems could stop bleeding when I watched an injured rabbit in my herb garden nibbling on them. The rabbit had a bad cut on its hind leg, bad enough to die from. I tried to catch it to bandage its leg, but it disappeared down a rabbit hole. I was very surprised to see it still alive the next day, and still nibbling on dandelion stems. So I picked some and made them into a mash. I tried the mash on the gums of Dolor's patients and their bleeding stopped much sooner than usual." Linnea stopped abruptly and swatted at the red tail-feathers of Samson the parrot as he flew by. Samson had swooped down on Nikki and snatched the piece of toast she was eating right out of her hand.

"Samson, I'm warning you," said Linnea, wagging her finger at him. "If you don't behave I'll lock you out of the house and you'll have to scrounge for your supper in the forest."

Samson just glared at her with his beady eyes as he came to rest on a dining chair, his sharp black claws digging into the carved wood. His powerful beak made quick work of the toast as it disappeared down his throat in a shower of crumbs. Nutter the chipmunk dashed out from under the dining table and hoovered up the crumbs like a tiny furry vacuum cleaner.

Linnea sighed. "I love animals, but Samson tries even my patience sometimes. He was a cute ball of feathers when he was a baby, but he gets meaner every year. Not only does he steal food, but he also likes to bite the fingers of my cook. I have to overpay the cook each week to keep him from leaving. Though Samson does make a very good watchdog, I'll say that for him. Once he attacked a robber who was breaking in through the kitchen window. Samson flew at the robber's face and scratched deep, bloody claw marks down his cheeks. I actually had to treat the robber's wounds, he was bleeding so much." She grinned at Nikki. "I made sure to use plenty of peppermint, to get the maximum stinging effect."

Fuzz guffawed as he wiped ale foam off his chin. "That's the way to treat crooks. Give 'em a good dose of pain and suffering."

Athena sniffed from her seat by the fireplace. "That is highly amusing, coming from someone who has stolen cherry tarts from every bakery in the Realm."

Fuzz shrugged and waved a careless hand. "That's not robbery. Bakers expect people to sample their wares. They should be flattered.

I'm helping their business by judging the flakiness of their crusts and the juiciness of their cherries. I should be charging them for my expert critiques."

Athena took a deep breath, about to respond loudly and in great detail. Fuzz sensed the danger.

He clapped his hands. "Okay everyone. All packed and ready? Good, let's head out." He left the cottage at a pace expertly calculated to out-run Athena's voice.

Nikki hitched up her rucksack and followed, grinning as she heard Athena mumbling behind her about certain greedy imps who were going to get fat from eating too many pies and gulping too much ale.

Their walk to the village near Linnea's cottage was pleasant enough, though they were constantly on the watch for Lurkers and palace guards.

Nikki kept feeling like they were being watched, but each time she turned to look at the dusty dirt road behind them no one was there.

The countryside was a mix of wheat fields and hills covered with fir trees and rhododendron bushes. Blackberry bushes lined the road, bursting with plump berries and tiny white flowers. Curio plucked handfuls of berries and soon his face and hands were as purple as the berries themselves. When he got tired of eating berries he pulled out a tiny knife Fuzz had given him and cut a slender branch from a birch tree at the side of the road.

"On guard!" he yelled, lunging at Fuzz and poking him in the stomach with the branch.

The branch bent as if it was rubber and flipped up, hitting Fuzz on the nose.

"Kid, you'll never make it as a swordsman," said Fuzz, rubbing his nose. "I suggest you give up now."

Curio ran back and forth across the road, making wild slashing motions with his branch. "You wait and see. I'm going to be a knight and I'll challenge that stinkpot Rufius to a duel. I'll drive him out of the Realm and then all the imps will be safe. I just need to practice." He jabbed his branch at a rabbit which had hopped out of the blackberry bushes. The rabbit dodged his blows, neatly side-stepping each attack. Its nose quivered as if daring Curio to try again.

Fuzz laughed. "See? Even the rabbits aren't afraid of you. Face it kid, you'll never be a fighter. You just don't have the bulk. You're barely imp-size."

"I'll be big when I'm grown up," said Curio, frowning and crossing his arms, nearly hitting himself in the face with his branch.

Fuzz shook his head. "I don't think so, kid. You're a shrimp, even for a ten-year-old. But your brains aren't half bad. If I were you, I'd apprentice yourself to someone like Gwen here. Learn a useful trade."

Gwen looked a bit surprised at this, but she put an arm around Curio. "You're welcome to learn from me, if you'd like. Once this problem with Rufius is settled we can both go back to Deceptionville and set up shop. Despite its faults that's the best place in the Realm for practical-minded people like you and me. I'll repair all the broken bridges, plows, and wagons in town by day and work on my experiments at night. And you can run errands to start with. When you're old enough I'll show you how to smelt iron and mix substances in my laboratory."

Curio brushed away a tear with a filthy sleeve. "Thank you, Miss. That would be real nice. Almost like having a home. And I bet you won't beat me like my old master used to. Though you can if you want to."

"Of course I'm not going to beat you, you silly ninny," said Gwen. "Do you honestly expect everyone you meet to beat you?"

Curio shrugged. "My master used to say it was good for little boys. Kept 'em in line and gave 'em a tough skin." He pulled up his pant leg. The scars on his shin bone twisted around his leg like white ropes.

Gwen gasped and tears sprouted in her eyes. "Oh, Curio," she said, pulling him into a hug. "How awful. I'm so sorry."

Curio hugged her back and then dashed away down the road, swinging his stick at imaginary knights and whistling out of tune.

WHEN THEY REACHED the main square of the village they found the road blocked. A crowd was clustered around the village bakery, which was a large stone building on one side of the square. The top half of the bakery's chimney had collapsed. It had come crashing down onto the cobblestones of the main street, leaving a gaping hole in the side of the building. The village children, not to mention the village chickens, were snatching up the smashed pies and pastries which littered the street.

They joined a group of villagers who were watching workmen haul on a rope attached to a pulley. The pulley dangled from a rickety wooden scaffold and the workmen were trying to guide a massive stone into a tricky angle between the remains of the chimney and a brick oven.

"They're using a two-wheel pulley," said Gwen, her hands on her hips, her eyes following the swinging stone. "I would have used a four-wheel. It creates much more lifting force with less effort."

Nikki nodded as she watched more workmen rush over to help. There were now eight men sweating and straining as they pulled on the rope, but they were still having trouble lifting the stone. It swayed dangerously on the thin rope and the villagers all took a nervous step backwards away from the scaffolding.

Nikki tried to recall what she'd learned about pulleys in her AP Physics class. A one-wheel pulley was just a rope slung over a grooved metal or wooden wheel. It didn't help lessen the effort of lifting something. If you used a one-wheel pulley to lift a one-hundred-pound stone, you'd have to pull on the rope with a hundred pounds of force. Using a two-wheel pulley, on the other hand, would decrease your effort by half. If you needed to lift a one-hundred-pound stone you'd only have to pull on the rope with fifty pounds of force. This decrease in effort was called a mechanical advantage, and a two-wheel pulley had a mechanical advantage of two.

A four-wheel pulley had a mechanical advantage of four. You'd only need to pull with twenty-five pounds of force to lift a one-hundred-pound stone. She'd asked her physics teacher why she'd never seen a pulley with twenty or even more wheels. It seemed like that would reduce the effort to almost zero. But her teacher had explained that pulleys were very similar to levers. To decrease the effort you had to increase the length. In the case of a lever like a seesaw you lengthened the board. If you sat on the very end of a long seesaw you could lift a very heavy person who was sitting on the other end, provided they were sitting near the fulcrum, or balancing point. Your distance from the fulcrum gave you more lifting power and cancelled out their weight to some extent. Pulleys had a similar length versus lifting-force problem. For pulleys you had to lengthen the rope attached to the wheels. A twenty-wheel pulley would require a ridiculously long rope. Instead of standing near the thing you wanted to lift you'd have to stand blocks or even miles away. That was why in her world manual pulleys were no longer used to lift very heavy things like steel girders. Human power had been replaced by gasoline-powered or electric-powered engines which could lift much more weight than a person pulling on a rope.

"I wonder why they aren't using a horse," said Gwen as the workmen strained to lift the heavy stone. "In Deceptionville they use teams of horses to lift very heavy stones, like the ones used in bridge-building. Though, come to think of it, I haven't seen any horses in this village. I wonder why. They're expensive to feed and stable, but even so most villages have at least one."

"The Knights of the Iron Fist have taken all of the horses near Kingston for their own use," said Linnea, joining them. "Ours were taken last year. The Knights used to leave the owners some compensation, a little gold, or a few sacks of wheat, but lately they just take the horses and throw the owners in the dungeon of the Southern Castle if they dare to complain. Rufius has been handing out gold and land to the Knights ever since he arrived in Kingston and now they do pretty much whatever he commands. The Knights have been around for centuries and they used to have a reputation for being honest, but this new generation seems to have no problem accepting bribes."

Gwen's eyes flashed with anger. "Why doesn't anyone stand up to these thugs? If we don't do something soon it will be too late. They'll have a permanent hold on power and the rest of us will be crushed under their boots. Or under the hooves of their horses."

Linnea pointed at Athena and Fuzz, who were watching the workmen. "Someone *is* standing up to them. The imps. And it is very much to our shame that the rest of us are letting them take such a big risk. The imps have always been the most vulnerable members of our society, and now that Rufius is targeting them they're even more at risk."

"Well," said Gwen, "I don't know how much help I'll be, but I for one will stand with them."

"Me too," said Nikki, painfully aware that she sounded braver than she felt. It didn't seem likely that the imps and their few support-ers could possibly stand up to Maleficious, Rufius, the palace guards, and the Knights of the Iron Fist. It seemed to her that Fuzz and Athena were counting too much on whatever influence the King and the Prince of Physics still had. She hoped she was wrong.

A plaintive mewling came from within her rucksack. Nikki bent down and scraped a piece of smashed blueberry pie off of the cobblestoned street. She reached behind her and held out the piece of pie until she felt a whiskery face snatch it and drag it down into the rucksack's depths. She didn't dare let Cation out just then. There were chickens all around them, pecking at the smashed pastries.

Knowing Cation she'd have no hesitation in pouncing on a full-grown chicken. Nikki wasn't sure who would win in a kitten-versus-chicken throw down, but she didn't want to find out.

Nikki wandered over to a work table someone had set up in the middle of the town square. The table was just a couple of boards laid across two sawhorses. It was covered with tools and scraps of parchment. She picked up a triangle made of metal with little tick-marks on its edges. Its center had been removed to form an interior triangle with a right angle of 90 degrees and two 45 degree angles. She recognized it as a set square. She'd used one made of plastic in her geometry class in junior high. Architects used them to create blueprints for buildings.

"What's that, Miss?" asked Curio, appearing at her elbow.

"It's called a set square," said Nikki, sighing as she looked down at the little boy. They had tried to leave Curio behind. The plan Fuzz was hatching was too dangerous for a child to be involved in. Linnea had offered to take him in, but he'd insisted on going with them. Athena had told her in private that they were planning on leaving Curio on Griff's ship once they reached Kingston, but Nikki was pretty sure that wasn't going to work. She had no doubt that Curio could sneak off a ship in a heartbeat.

"What's it for?" asked Curio, putting his arm through the hole in the middle of the set square and twirling it around so that it was a blur of metal. "Is it a weapon? I bet I could throw it a long way."

Nikki snatched it back just as he tried to put this theory into action. "It's not a weapon, it's a tool. The stonecutters who are fixing the bakery are using it to measure angles and to make straight lines, so that their blocks of stone fit together." She pointed at the scattered parchments on the work table. "See? The master stonecutter used it to draw these plans for the new chimney."

"What's this mean?" asked Curio, pointing with a grubby finger at a note on the bottom of a scrap of parchment which read "1 nail =

10 hands".

Nikki frowned at it. "I'm not sure."

"It's a scale marker," said Gwen, joining them.

"Oh, of course" said Nikki. "Like those scales you see on maps: 1 inch equals 1 mile."

"Here in the Realm one nail means the length of one thumbnail," said Gwen. She pointed at her own thumbnail. "Not a very exact measurement, obviously. The length of my thumbnail is only about half the length of the thumbnail of a large man. The builders in Deceptionville have been trying for years to agree on a more stand-ardized measure, but they haven't come to any agreement yet."

"So, a 'hand', is that . . .?" Nikki waved her right hand.

"Yes," said Gwen. "It's the length of your hand from your wrist to the tip of your middle finger. Obviously, using hand length as a measurement is even more of a problem than using thumbnails." She gestured at the parchments scattered across the work table. "All these detailed building plans are great, but without standardized measure-ments the finished buildings have a lot of structural problems. As you can see," she said pointing at the collapsed chimney. "The King was supposed to convene a gathering of builders at Castle Cogent last year, to agree on a list of standard measurements for length and weight, but the meeting never took place. I think the King just got bored with the idea, as he does with so many things." She sighed. "I've never met him, but I've heard that the King is a nice man. It's good to be nice, but sometimes I wish the King was a little less nice and a little more hard-working. Laziness in a ruler can be dangerous. It's a weakness which evil people like Rufius can exploit. The King is too lazy to do the hard work of running the Realm, so Rufius offers to step in and do the job himself. The King lets him just to save himself the bother of all that work."

"Aye, the King should spend a day breaking rock in the Kingston quarry. After the tenth blister on 'is palms and the tenth bruise on 'is shins he'll think a bit o' paperwork and tax collecting is a party."

Nikki and Gwen looked up at the man who'd joined them at the work table. Nikki guessed that he wasn't much older than Gwen, maybe twenty-five or so. But he had the sunburned skin and grey hair of a much older man, and his hands and arms were crossed with dozens of scars. He was staring at Gwen with unabashed appreciation.

"Where are me manners," he said, wiping his hand on his rough woolen shirt before offering it to Gwen. "Name's Darius. I'm the head stonecutter 'round these parts."

Gwen shook his hand a bit warily, giving him a searching look with her blue eyes. "Pleased to meet you," she said. "These are my friends, Nikki and Curio."

Darius nodded at Nikki but didn't offer to shake hands, probably because he was still holding Gwen's.

"So, you drew up these plans?" said Gwen, pulling her hand out of his grasp and picking up a piece of parchment from the work table. "I would have gone with a thirty-five degree angle here where the chimney meets the wall of the bakery, not a twenty-five degree one. The steeper angle would have reduced the stress on the load-bearing beams on that side of the building."

Darius raised an eyebrow and ran a dirty hand through his hair. "What're ye saying? That me design brought down the chimney? Because meself and me crew did repair work on that blasted chimney only last year."

"No, I'm not saying that," said Gwen quickly. "Judging by the bricks scattered all over the town square I'd guess that the chimney is at least one-hundred years old. Old bricks will crumble, despite the best building designs in the world." She bent down and picked up a piece of brick off the cobblestones. A greyish material was attached to one side of the brick. Gwen rubbed it with her finger and it crumbled into dust. "It looks like the chimney was built using clay mortar," she said.

"Aye," said Darius. "We get our clay from a pit in the Haunted Hills. Makes the best mortar. Doesn't wash away in the rain as quickly as others."

"Hmm," said Gwen, setting the brick on the worktable. "I've been experimenting in my workshop in Deceptionville with a substance dug from the limestone cliffs along the coast, not far from here. When heated and then mixed with water and sand this substance makes a remarkably strong and waterproof mortar."

Nikki examined the tools on the workbench as Gwen and Darius talked. She hid a smile as she watched Darius hanging on Gwen's every word. She didn't want to interrupt, but she was pretty sure the substance Gwen was describing was called lime in her world. The Romans had used it to build bridges and aqueducts. Her history teacher had described the lime-making process when they'd studied the Roman Empire. Lime was just crushed limestone. Limestone could be found all over the world in seaside cliffs and was made out of the shells of clams and oysters, as well as the bones of fish which had collected at the bottom of the ocean for millions of years. If she remembered correctly, the shells and bones were made out of calcium carbonate. The Romans heated the lime and then mixed it with sand and water to form a sticky mortar which was waterproof and much stronger than earlier types of mortar. They spread it between bricks to hold them together the same way modern bricklayers used cement.

"Hey you lovebirds. Hate to break up the flirting, but we've got to get going."

Gwen turned bright red as she, Nikki, and Darius turned to find Fuzz grinning up at them wickedly.

"You two can make googly eyes at each other later," said Fuzz. "Linnea wants to make a quick stop in the village to see the tooth kid from last night and then we need to hotfoot it down the road. I've been chatting up the villagers, and they say Lurkers have been spotted nearby. From the sound of it they're Deceptionville creeps employed by Avaricious. They're probably not connected with Rufius. Still, I'd like us out of the area as soon as possible. With a bit of fast marching we should be safely hidden on Griff's ship by midnight."

"Hey! That's me property," said Darius as Fuzz snagged a goose quill, a small bottle of ink, and several pieces of blank parchment off of the work table.

Fuzz grinned up at him. "You shouldn't leave your property just lying around in the middle of the village square. You never know when a thief might wander by." He tucked the items into a small rucksack which Linnea had given him. "Athena's been complaining that she needs writing materials," he said in aside to Nikki. "Apparently she memorized every word you said about logical falsities or fallacies or whatever they were. She wants to write it all down again and have it copied by scribes in Kingston. She's going to have the copies sent to every school in the Realm. I told her she's wasting her time. People in the Realm are more likely to use parchment to light the fire for their supper than they are to read anything written on it. Athena's always been big on education, but most people just want full bellies, not full heads."

As Nikki followed Fuzz and the others through the back alleys of the village she mulled over Fuzz's comment about the Lurkers. Her last encounter with them had been in the dungeons of the Confounded Castle in the Haunted Hills. They'd captured her on the orders of Avaricious, who had the crackpot idea that she could somehow turn lead into gold. She wondered if Avaricious had sent them here to find her. She glanced back over her shoulder. Nothing but an empty cobblestoned street lined with half-timbered houses. A dog barked somewhere, and a goat was slowly wandering down the street chewing a half-eaten corncob. No creepy black-cloaked figures were anywhere in sight.

Whiskers tickled her neck. Nikki laughed and pulled Cation out of her rucksack. The kitten purred loudly and tried to balance on Nikki's shoulder.

"Ouch!" Nikki gently detached Cation's claws from the navy silk tunic Kira had given her in Kingston. "You're making me wish I had that blasted Seeker robe on. Bet you couldn't get your claws through that."

"Wait a sec, Miss," said Curio, who was walking beside her. He pulled out his tiny knife and sawed off a piece of fabric from the bottom of his pants leg. "Try this."

Nikki draped the fabric over her left shoulder and re-attached Cation. The kitten kneaded the fabric like bread dough then seemed to declare herself satisfied. She wrapped her tail around Nikki's neck and purred loudly in her ear.

"Thanks Curio," said Nikki. "Be careful with that knife."

"Don't worry, Miss," said Curio. "I'm used to knives. Always have one with me. You can use it for lots of things: cutting meat, whittling, sharpening goose quills, but mostly I used it back in Deceptionville for stabbing my master when he tried to beat me."

Nikki gasped.

"Oh, don't worry, Miss," said Curio. "I only stabbed him a little, in the arm. Mostly he was too drunk to even notice. He was a tough one. Permanently pickled, you might say."

"Here we are," said Linnea, stopping in front of a little wooden house which seemed to have more holes than wood in its walls. "My little patient from last night lives here. Why don't you all wait out here? It's a bit cramped in there. They've got twelve people living in two rooms. I'll just be a minute."

Curio sat down on an upturned bucket. Darius, who had followed Gwen all the way from the worksite in the town square, took off the leather tool belt he was wearing and set it on the cobblestones for Gwen to sit on. Fuzz and Athena positioned themselves at either end of the street, as lookouts.

Nikki, after a moment's hesitation, followed Linnea inside the rickety little house. She regretted her action almost immediately. The stench was overwhelming. It smelled like a dozen Porta-Potties had been tipped over. As her eyes adjusted to the dark room she realized that the smell came from several overflowing chamber pots under the unmade beds which took up half the room.

A tiny figure jumped up from one of the beds.

"Miss Linnea!" The little boy with the two missing front teeth ran to Linnea and hugged her tightly.

Linnea stroked his hair. "How are you feeling today? Any pain?" She felt his forehead. "No fever. That's a good sign."

"I'm fine, Miss. My teeth are bleeding a bit, but they don't hurt."

Linnea scrounged in her bag of herbs and pulled out a small glass jar with a cork stopper. "Rub this on your gums twice a day. The bleeding should stop completely by the day after tomorrow. If it doesn't come straight to my cottage and I'll apply a stronger version."

Wide-eyed, the little boy took the bottle and held it cupped in his hands like it was a magical potion.

"Is that the mixture of crushed dandelions you mentioned back in your cottage?" asked Nikki.

Linnea nodded. "This is a weak version. I used to use a much more concentrated version, but I noticed that the strong version would cause my older patients to have severe dizzy spells and chest pains."

Nikki nodded. She didn't know much about herbal medicine, but the dandelion mixture Linnea was using probably contained vitamin K. Vitamin K helped blood to clot, which stopped someone who had a deep cut from bleeding to death. Nikki guessed that if you gave too much of it to elderly people it could cause a large blood clot which could cause a stroke or a heart attack. She shuddered, wondering how close Linnea had ever come to killing someone. Herbal medicine was better than nothing she supposed, but she was very glad her world had progressed beyond herbs to modern, well-tested drugs and medical procedures. She knew some kids in her high school back in Wisconsin who swallowed herbal supplements as if they were candy, but she thought that was insane. With herbs and supplements you never knew exactly what you were getting, or how much of an active substance you were getting. Just like Linnea's dandelion mixture, you might be getting a useful substance like vitamin K, but the amount could vary wildly. Not just due to the expertise of the potion-mixer, but also due to factors like what kind of soil the dandelions grew in.

The little boy had uncorked the bottle and was cautiously sniffing its contents. "It was very kind of you to come see me, Miss Linnea," he said. "But you and your friends best not stay." He looked around the room as if spotting dark forces in every corner. "*They've* been here."

"Knights or Lurkers?" asked Linnea at once.

"Lurkers, Miss. And they've been searching for a girl with long dark hair who wears strange clothes and travels with two imps." He looked up at Nikki curiously. "Are you a furriner, Miss? I've never met any. My Pa went to Kingston once, to sell a pig. He said there were furriners there who sailed into port from faraway lands. He said some of 'em had two heads and some others had blue skin." He stared hard at Nikki's neck, as if expecting it to suddenly sprout another head.

"We should go," said Linnea. She gave the boy a last pat on the head and hustled Nikki toward the door. Before they could leave a shadow blocked the doorway.

Nikki froze. The man in the doorway looked like the twin of the one she'd seen in Deceptionville. The one who'd been watching Gwen's gunpowder experiment. He was tall, pale, and wearing a black cloak with the hood pulled up. Despite her shock Nikki had a sudden urge to laugh. The hood reminded her of the hoodies boys at her high school wore to seem tough.

As he stepped toward Nikki a demon seemed to erupt from her

shoulder. Cation sprang from her perch and launched herself at the man's face. The kitten's hissing, spitting and yowling echoed around the room.

The man cursed and clutched at the kitten as her sharp claws drew blood.

"Run Miss Linnea!" yelled the little boy, throwing himself on the ground in front of the man's feet. The man tripped and fell face-first to the floor.

Cation detached her claws from his face and jumped aside. Nikki scooped her up and dashed out into the street.

"Lurkers!" shouted Linnea. "Everyone follow me!"

Fuzz and Athena sprinted from their lookout posts, Darius lifted Gwen to her feet and snatched up his toolbelt. Curio whipped out his tiny knife, eyeing the fallen Lurker like a chef about to carve up a turkey.

"Not now, Curio," gasped Nikki, grabbing his arm and pulling him into the alley Linnea had disappeared down.

Linnea obviously knew every street and alley in the village. They ran close on her heels as she led them through back gardens and empty stables and through a courtyard where women were washing laundry by beating the wet clothes with wooden paddles. Nikki grabbed Athena just in time as the imp slipped on the soapy water and nearly fell into a laundry tub.

"Thank you, Miss," gasped Athena. "I'm not as nimble as I used to be." She gathered up the skirt of her grey dress and dashed after Linnea, who was nearly out of sight.

Linnea didn't let them stop running until they'd reached the far edge of town. She pushed through a thicket of blackberry bushes growing by the side of the road. The tangled curtain of thorns hid a narrow path through the endless dunes of blackberries. They followed the path away from the road and up a steep hill.

"Rest here for a bit," gasped Linnea. "I think we've lost him."

They all collapsed onto a little patch of damp grass surrounded by bushes. Nikki set Cation down on the grass and surveyed the damage the blackberry thorns had done. Her jeans had survived but her silk tunic had several long rips in the sleeves. Good thing she still had her Westlake Debate Team T-shirt on underneath. If she ever saw Kira again she might have to ask for some new clothes.

Fuzz was peering out through the blackberry bushes. "I can see a good stretch of the road, and I don't think there's anyone on it. Course, he could always come at us from another direction. Lurkers are notorious for knowing every road, alleyway and deer path in the Realm."

Everyone immediately looked over their shoulder at the wall of bushes behind them.

Linnea shook her head. "Nobody could get through that mess of thorns. This area is the village's prime berry-picking spot for a reason. These blackberry bushes cover a good five miles, deep into the countryside on both sides of the road. Locals like myself know a few paths through the thorns, but an outsider would have to use the road. And that Lurker is definitely an outsider. Our little village isn't important enough to have a Lurker stationed in it. Even if he comes from somewhere close, like Kingston, he wouldn't know our blackberry paths." She sighed. "I wasn't planning a trip to Kingston. It's not my favorite place. I prefer the peace of the countryside to the noise and crowds of a big city. But it looks like I don't have much choice. You need a local guide to get you to Kingston's port without this dratted Lurker spotting you."

Darius cleared his throat and glanced sideways at Gwen. "I could guide 'em. Seeing as how I'm a local, same as yourself."

Linnea harrumphed. "No disrespect stonecutter, but you spend all your time in the rock quarry, breaking big stones into small ones. You don't know the land hereabouts like I do. I've scoured the land for herbs and seeds from here to Kingston. I know every rock and tree, every hill and every valley for miles around."

Darius nodded slowly. "Fair point. But if we do meet up with a Lurker, or even one of them tin-headed Knights, I wager I can pound him into a bloody lump a lot easier than you can." He pulled a small sledge-hammer out of his toolbelt and bashed an imaginary knight with it.

"Excellent!" said Fuzz. "So that's settled then. You're both coming with us to Kingston. I'm sure Griff has room for two more on her ship."

Linnea and Darius both looked a bit startled at their sudden recruitment into the group, but they didn't raise any objections. Linnea took charge and decided they wouldn't leave their hiding place among the blackberry bushes until after dark. Everyone stretched out on the grass, scratching at the places where the thorns had ripped through their clothes.

"Aargh!" exclaimed Fuzz, rubbing at the red marks on the sleeve of his shirt. "Is there anything in that bag of yours to sooth an itch?" he asked Linnea. "It feels like I've been boxing with a gang of angry bees."

Linnea scrounged in her bag of herbs and potions, pulling out bottles, jars and bunches of dried plants. "I have these," she said, pulling out a fresh bunch of daisy-like flowers. "They relieve itching, but they need to be dried, crushed and mixed with linseed oil. The fresh flowers won't do you much good, I'm afraid."

While Fuzz scratched and muttered irritably Nikki pulled one of the flowers out of the bunch. It was chamomile. The herb garden behind her high school had a big patch of these growing under a birch tree. Her biology class sometimes spent class time tending the garden, which was a big hit with everyone. It was much better to be outside digging in the dirt and seeing real plants than to be inside staring at pictures of plants in a textbook. In addition to the chamomile they grew lavender, basil, arnica, nettles, and comfrey. The dopers kept asking their teacher, Mrs. Beattie, if they could grow a marijuana plant. Mrs. Beattie would just smile each time they asked and make them shovel the organic fertilizer they used on the garden. Fertilizer-shoveling was not a popular job. The stuff was mostly made out of fresh cow poop and smelled exactly like you'd expect fresh cow poop to smell.

Nikki twirled the flower between her fingers. She tried to remember the Linnaean classification for chamomile, but all she could remember was the family name, Asteraceae. The Asteraceae family contained asters, sunflowers, and daisies. She was pretty sure the genus was Aster, but she couldn't remember the species. She knew asters and daisies were members of the huge category of flowering plants called Angiosperms. Angiosperms had first appeared in the Triassic period, about 200 million years ago. They differed from the older class of plants called Gymnosperms because Angiosperms had flowers while Gymnosperms had cones, like the pinecones on a pine tree. She closed her eyes, trying to remember the rest of the classification for chamomile, but couldn't. She sighed. She had a good memory, but the Realm was really straining it to the utmost. You didn't realize how dependent you were on Google until you found yourself in a land where Google-like stuff wouldn't be invented for centuries. Eyes still closed, she yawned widely. All this running through the countryside was making her sleepy. She slipped her shoulders out of her rucksack and curled in a ball on the grass. As she was dozing off she felt Cation's tiny claws kneading her back. She fell asleep to the kitten's purring.

Chapter Five

Gunpowder and Greed

"WHAT THE . . . ?" Nikki sat bolt upright, heart pounding. She was in the back of a wagon, jolting along a dirt road. The night sky was pitch black, with just the tiniest sliver of a moon shining through the trees on the side of the road. Dry straw crackled underneath her. There was a strange taste in her mouth, and her head felt like it was stuffed with cotton.

"Well, look who's finally awake."

Nikki gasped as the faint moonlight shone on what looked like a skeleton dressed in rags. The skeleton was sitting on a raised wooden platform at the front of the wagon. It seemed to be holding the reins of two black horses. The skeleton turned its head to look at her and Nikki breathed a tiny sigh of relief. It was Dolor, the toothpuller from last night. Dolor wasn't someone you wanted to meet on a dark road, but he was better than a skeleton.

Dolor chuckled. "I don't know much, maybe, but two things I do know are teeth and blackberry paths. I like a tasty pie now and then, and I pick the juiciest berries myself. Linnea's not the only one who knows the way through that sea of thorns."

Nikki edged away from him. She didn't know why she was in this wagon with Dolor, but she didn't want to just sit there waiting to find out. Whatever the reason it was bound to be unpleasant. Maybe she could jump off and run for the cover of the trees before he could catch her. She stretched a hand out to steady herself but found her hand stuck in mid-air. An iron band around her wrist clinked. It was bolted to the side of the wagon.

Dolor's laughter ripped the night air like a rusty saw. "Not going anywhere, you are. Quite a nice surprise it was, seeing how easy you was to catch. I just dropped a rag soaked in nightshade on your face. The others never even woke up. Just snored away fit to raise the dead. For a bunch of people with Lurkers after 'em you sure don't keep much of a lookout."

Dolor spat over the side of the wagon. "Tried nightshade meself once. Stole a bottle from Linnea's pantry. That woman's too trusting. Never locks her door. Would've gotten away scot free but for that damned parrot of hers. He put up a fight, let me tell you. Squawked fit to raise the dead and gave me a gash on me arm that bled for days."

Nikki pulled on the iron chain. Only her left wrist was chained to the wagon. She put both feet on the side of the wagon and pulled as hard as she could on the chain with her right hand. The boards creaked, but her wrist remained firmly attached to them.

Dolor flicked the reins and the two black horses broke into a trot. "Headed to D-ville, we are. And the sooner we get there the better. Don't want that blasted Lurker tracking us down. Big price on your head, there is." He laughed again. "That fool Lurker was offering two gold coins to anyone in the village tavern who had news of you. Didn't take me long to realize that Avaricious had hired him. Avaricious runs all the Lurkers in D-ville. They're practically his own private little army. He used to be just a fat, greedy lump of a pig, but word is he's gotten a taste for power. Got hisself a seat on the town council now. Trying to set up his own little kingdom in D-ville. Wonder what that young slimeball Rufius thinks about that. He's the power round these parts. Got his dainty foot on the neck of the poor saps in Kingston, he does. Next thing you know he'll be kicking the Prince out of his fancy mansion and the King out of his castle." Dolor shrugged. "Avaricious and Rufius can go at each other's throats like rabid dogs in the street for all I care. Me, I just want a shiny little pile of gold. Enough so's I can retire from the tooth-pulling trade. Getting too old for it. Don't enjoy the screaming like I used to."

Nikki's teeth rattled as the wagon bounced along the rutted road. She glanced back. They were headed away from everyone she knew in the Realm, and she felt the familiar sinking feeling in her stomach. She was alone again in a strange world.

"TEN GOLD COINS. That's the only offer I'll make you." Avaricious stepped out of the doorway of his Deceptionville shop and shook a bag of coins in Dolor's face.

Dolor looked daggers at him as he jumped down from the wagon. "Living up to yer reputation, aren't you? Knew you'd try to skimp on the reward, you worthless lump of lard."

Avaricious shrugged. "If you'd brought me the blonde girl your reward would have been double."

"Well I didn't know you wanted her, did I?" said Dolor. He snatched the bag from Avaricious and held it under the light from a nearby torch to count the coins. "Your Lurker was going round the local taverns, asking for news of a dark-haired girl from foreign parts. Not my fault he didn't say nothing about no blonde girl."

Avaricious ignored his grumblings and jerked an impatient finger at the iron band around Nikki's wrist. Dolor took his sweet time searching his pockets for the key, but he finally released Nikki from the chain. The two hooded Lurkers behind Avaricious pulled Nikki from the wagon and hustled her into Avaricious's workshop.

Nikki's nose wrinkled as the familiar smell of unvented chemicals wafted around her. They marched her past the smoke and steam of the smelters pouring their liquid metals, and past the benches of the alchemists sending up sparks and stenches from their glass bottles heated by oil lamps. Nikki expected them to take her to the bench she'd unwillingly worked at weeks before, but instead they hauled her up a narrow set of stairs lined with dusty tapestries. The heavy footsteps and labored breathing of Avaricious followed behind them.

"In there," she heard Avaricious say.

The Lurkers dragged her into a room and left her standing on a faded rug with a picture of a white horse woven into it. They retreated to guard the doorway and Avaricious pushed past them. He stopped in front of Nikki and folded his ring-encrusted hands on his fat belly.

"You'll work, eat and sleep in here until you produce what I want," he said, nodding to the bed in one corner, a small wooden table with a jug of water and basket of wormy apples on it, and a large workbench in front of the barred window. "If you need any ingredients just write them on a piece of folded parchment and drop it in there." He pointed to a brass pipe which came up through the floor and opened at knee-height into a shape like a calla lily. "That goes straight to my stockroom. They'll deliver anything you need."

Nikki glared at him and crossed her blackberry-scratched arms. "I don't understand. What is it you want me to do?"

"Don't worry," said Avaricious, waving a lazy hand. "No more attempts to turn lead into gold. Not for you, anyway. I have a few of my best alchemists still working on that, but I'm beginning to think it's hopeless. No, I want something else. Something more likely to succeed. I want you to make me some of that exploding powder one of my Lurkers saw that blonde girl make. It's her I really want, of course, but she's disappeared and my Lurkers can find no trace of her. They searched her dwelling but found no instructions on how to make this wonderful powder. You were there when she demonstrated it, and you have some knowledge of alchemy. You will recreate her discovery or you will stay in this room until you die." He turned on his heel and left the room.

Nikki winced as she heard the bolt slam home. The door was a thick slab of oak and the hinges were on the other side. No chance of getting out that way. She turned immediately to the window, but any hope she had of escaping was soon dashed. Unlike the open window she'd escaped through at Confounded Castle this window was barred with heavy iron rods which were secured to the stone wall with bolts as large as her thumb.

She sighed and took a cautious sip from the jug of water. It was stale, but seemed safe to drink. She doubted that Avaricious would drug or poison her. He needed her alive and alert to make his exploding powder. She flopped back onto the thin woolen spread covering the bed, sending up a small cloud of dust.

Exploding powder. Gunpowder. A lot of things had scared her since she'd arrived in the Realm. Maleficious had sent a shiver up her spine, that first day at Castle Cogent, with his dark eyes glaring at her from under his bushy white eyebrows. Fortuna and her greedy fortune-telling scam had been a little bit scary. Avaricious was way ahead of Fortuna in the greed department, and his lust for money made him dangerous. Dolor was scary in a creepy, haunted-house sort of way. And Rufius, with his weirdly clean clothes and his lust for power was the scariest person she'd met so far in the Realm. But gunpowder scared her more than any of them. Nikki clenched her jaw determinedly. She was *not* going to be the person who introduced guns and gunpowder to the Realm.

She closed her eyes and tried to block the memories of two years ago, but they came flooding in anyway. Three kids had died. Two girls and a boy. All of them only twelve years old. They went to her junior high, but she hadn't known anyone of them well. Still, their faces were burned into her memory. Their pictures had been on the front page of the Westlake Journal. The headline had been 'Shooter at Westlake Junior High. Three dead.'

She'd been out on the school soccer field when it happened, warming up for a practice game. She heard the shots, but hadn't really known what they were until her soccer coach yelled at the team to run toward the far end of the field. They'd run all the way off the school grounds and into a nearby restaurant, where her coach had called 911.

Nikki hadn't learned about the deaths until the next day. Her mother had kept her home from school and tearfully showed her the newspaper. A local boy, only a teenager himself, had taken an assault weapon from his father's hoard of guns and sprayed the halls of her junior high school with bullets. In addition to the three deaths more than thirty kids had been wounded. The mother of one of the dead girls had committed suicide a few days later, unable to bear her grief. No one in the town really knew why the killer done it. There was a lot of wild guesses, but no real proof. Some people said he played a lot of violent shooter-type video games. Some people said he was on drugs. But no one ever really knew for sure. He killed himself before the police caught him.

Nikki had never thought much about guns before that. Her mother certainly never owned any. None of her friends' parents did either, as far as she knew. But after the shooting she thought about guns a lot. She thought about them all the time, for more than a year afterward. Guns had suddenly become something she couldn't ignore. After the shooting she hated guns more than anything else on the entire planet.

And now here she was in the Realm, a world without guns, and someone was expecting her to make gunpowder. Nikki snorted. Well, *that* wasn't going to happen. She glanced over at the brass tube sticking up out of the floor. She supposed she could drop parchments down it, requesting random ingredients. Avaricious and the people in his stockroom didn't know what ingredients were needed for gunpowder. She could do what she'd done the last time she'd been in Avaricious's workshop: fake it.

Her eyebrows knit together in a frown. Guns might not exist in the Realm, but there was another person here who knew how to make gunpowder. Gwen. She'd tried to talk Gwen out of experimenting with gunpowder, back in Gwen's front yard, when the Lurker had seen her test explosion. But she wasn't sure she'd gotten through to Gwen. Gwen had been intent on using the powder for engineering purposes like building tunnels. Her exploding powder could save huge amounts of time and manual labor when trying to build a tunnel through a mountain. But Gwen hadn't really thought about the powder's more dangerous possibilities, like using it to make weapons.

The worst thing about Gwen's discovery was that Rufius knew about it. That was why he'd had Gwen locked up in the Southern Castle in Kingston. And when Gwen had escaped by blasting through the castle wall Rufius had seen for himself just how destructive gunpowder could be. He was probably sitting in the Southern Castle this very moment, deciding what to blow up. Nikki bet that one of the things on his list was the King's treasury. Athena had mentioned that both Castle Cogent and the Southern Castle had super-secure rooms filled with gold bars and bags of gold coins. They were for use by the King in bad times, when crops failed and the people of the Realm were hungry. The King could use the treasury to buy food from other lands.

Nikki shuddered. The power of the King would crumble if Rufius or Avaricious got hold of the treasury. They would use the gold to bribe people, the way Rufius had bribed the Knights of the Iron Fist to rebel against the King, to bully the people of Kingston, and to attack the imp headquarters in the Trackless Forest. Power was what Rufius wanted, even a foreigner like herself could see that. With the gold in the treasury Rufius could set himself up as King.

Not if she could help it. Nikki jumped up from the bed and grabbed a piece of parchment off the work bench. She dipped a quill in an ink pot and thought for a second, rubbing her nose with the feathered end of the pen. She glanced at the iron bars on the window. Avaricious' storeroom was sure to have acids. Hydrochloric acid, or maybe nitric acid, would probably do the trick. She was pretty sure that one of them would dissolve iron, or the stone which the iron bars of the window were bolted to. She hesitated, her quill hovering over the parchment. What would people in the Realm call these substances? Hydrochloric acid got its name because it was a solution of hydrogen and chloride dissolved in water. It had been discovered by the alchemist Jabir ibn Hayyan around 800 AD. But it hadn't gotten its modern name until much later, around 1818, when the English chemist Humphry Davy proved that it was composed of hydrogen and chlorine. The Realm wasn't advanced enough to know about atoms, molecules, or the periodic table. They would still be using older, alchemy-type names for these substances. She knew that alchemists in the middle ages in her world had used acids to dissolve gold. They'd called the acids 'spirits' or 'salt spirits'. She wrote that on the parchment. For good measure she also wrote 'acid' and 'dissolving liquids'. She folded the parchment and dropped it down the brass tube. A few seconds later she heard three loud bangs on the pipe. That must mean the storeroom had received her request. She grabbed an apple from the basket and sat back down on the bed to wait.

She'd eaten three apples, and probably a few worms, when she heard voices outside the door. She jumped up from the bed just as the door creaked open. A short, bald man wearing a leather smock with burn marks all over it entered the room. He was carrying a silver tray.

"Here you are young Miss, just as you requested."

The man carefully set the tray down on the workbench and stepped back, smiling and nodding at Nikki.

Nikki regarded him warily and then slowly approached the workbench. The tray held a selection of glass bottles stoppered with corks.

The man waved a hand as if presenting an array of fabulous jewels. "Our finest spirits, straight from the distillers."

"Um," said Nikki, "you realize that I meant alchemic dissolving liquids, don't you? Not spirits that you drink, like vodka or gin."

The man gave a high-pitched chuckle which made Nikki wonder about his sanity.

"Not sure what vodka is, young Miss, but I can personally assure you that these are the finest dissolving liquids you could ask for." He tapped one of the bottles with his finger. "I distilled this one myself. We use it for dissolving gold. Called King's Sorrow, it is. For what King wants his gold dissolved into a puddle?" He gave another shriek of a chuckle.

Nikki took a quick step back from him. "Okay. Well, if you could just leave them here I'll get to work."

The man rubbed his bald head with a hand that was an odd shade of grayish-white. "I was hoping you'd let me watch you work, young Miss. Rumors are flying that old Avaricious is trying to concoct some sort of new substance that does wonderful things. The boys down in the iron smelter say that it will make you light as a feather, so you can just float along down the street like a wisp of a cloud." Small flakes of white drifted off of his hands as he waved them in the air.

Nikki bent down and picked one of the white flakes off the floor. "What is this? Some kind of hand cream?"

The man let out an ear-piercing shriek of laughter. "Hand cream. If that's not a good joke then I don't know what is. Yes, it's just me and the fancy ladies in the King's court up at Castle Cogent, putting on our rose-scented creams. No, young Miss. That's lead paste we mix up here in the shop. The potters use it on their cups and plates before they go into the kiln. Gives dishes a nice shiny coating."

Nikki stared at him, her mouth hanging open. "And you mix this paste without using any gloves? It gets all over your hands?"

The man shrugged. "Don't need gloves, not for this stuff. It's harmless. I've been mixing it since I was apprenticed to Avaricious at age ten." He pulled a pair of thick leather gloves from his belt. "Nope, you don't need any gloves for paste-mixing, but these dissolving liquids, well, they're another story. I'll leave these gloves here for you. Be sure to put them on before you open any of these bottles. The pottery paste might turn your hands a bit ghostly white like mine, but these dissolving liquids will burn a hole right through you."

"But, the lead," said Nikki. "It's also very dangerous. You really shouldn't let it touch your skin. It can get into your blood and poison you."

The man let out another high-pitched cackle. "Goodness, young Miss, you certainly are a worrier, aren't you? If everyone here at the shop was like you we'd never get anything done. We'd have to close up the place and go home." He dropped the gloves on the workbench and headed for the door, still chuckling. He rapped on the door and it opened from the outside. He left with a last wave at Nikki and the bolt slammed home again.

Nikki stood staring at the door. Mixing lead paste by hand since he was ten years old. She shuddered. No wonder he seemed crazy. He probably was. Mental problems were a well-known side-effect of lead poisoning. She wondered how many other people in the Realm were exposed to high levels of lead. If they were using lead glazes on their dishes then the number of cases of lead poisoning was probably in the thousands. She wasn't sure how lead affected adults, but it was very toxic to young children.

She wandered absent-mindedly over to the bed and sat down. Someone should spread the word through the Realm about the dangers of lead. If someone who worked in Avaricious' shop every day didn't know about the danger then it was unlikely that the general public did. Her first thought was Athena. She was sure she could get the imp to understand the danger. But Athena, and the imps in general, didn't have much power or influence in the Realm. It was unlikely that people would listen to an imp. The King? No. He had power and influence, but he never seemed to take anything seriously.

The Prince of Physics? That was a much better idea. He had power, especially in Kingston. People would listen to him. Linnea was another person who could help. People already went to her for health problems. She would be an ideal person to spread the word not to eat or drink off of lead-glazed pottery, and not to touch lead with your bare hands. Lead poisoning from water pipes wasn't a problem, at least. The Realm didn't have plumbing yet. The only water pipes she'd seen in the Realm had been in the mansion of the Prince of Physics, and those had been copper.

Nikki sighed and stood up. Public health problems in the Realm would have to wait. She couldn't very well spread the word about the dangers of lead while she was locked in this room. She went back to the workbench and stood with her hands on her hips, staring down at the bottles on the silver tray. There was no way to tell what kinds of acids might be in the bottles just by looking at them. She eyed the bottle that was called King's Sorrow. According to her visitor it could dissolve gold, but gold was much softer than iron. She was probably going to need something stronger. Hydrochloric acid would dissolve iron. It was a clear liquid, like water. She bent down and squinted at the bottles. It was hard to tell, since some of the bottles were made of greenish glass, but it looked like most of the liquids had a yellowish tint. Only two of the liquids looked clear.

Nikki hesitated. Acids could be harmful to your lungs. She didn't want to open all the bottles and smell them. She wasn't sure what hydrochloric acid smelled like anyway. Well, she couldn't stand there all day just staring at bottles. She pulled on the heavy leather gloves and picked up a bottle containing clear liquid. She slowly eased its cork out and sniffed. The smell wafting from the open bottle was very sharp and made her eyes water. Trying not to breathe, she carried the bottle over to the window and poured a little of the liquid onto one of the iron bolts holding the bars in place.

She re-corked the bottle and stood back. The liquid on the bolt started to bubble, so there was definitely a chemical reaction taking place. She couldn't tell whether or not the liquid was actually dissolving the bolt. It would probably take some time. She uncorked the bottle again and poured the liquid on the rest of the bolts. A rusty smell filled the room. She glanced at the door. She knew there was a guard there. She could hear him shuffle his feet and clear his throat every once in a while.

She carefully corked the empty bottle and replaced it on the silver tray. Rolling up the rug with the picture of the white horse on it, she quietly dragged it in front of the door. Hopefully that would block the smell and keep the guard from investigating.

TWENTY MINUTES. IT was hard to estimate time without a watch or a clock, but Nikki was pretty sure the acid had been working on the bolts for at least twenty minutes. She pulled the dusty bedspread off the bed and carefully spread it out beneath the window. An experimental tug on the bars made her heart leap. They were loose!

She tugged harder and nearly cried out as two of the heavy bolts came loose from the wall and fell to the floor. A dull thud echoed around the room. Nikki glanced over her shoulder at the door. It stayed closed. The bedspread had muffled the sound enough. She tried to hold up the grid of iron bars with one hand while pulling out the bolts with the other, but the bars were too heavy. She was just going to have to chance it. She grabbed the bars with both hands and pulled with all her might.

The creaking and grating of metal sounded horribly loud as the entire grid of iron bars suddenly came loose from the wall. Nikki staggered under the weight, trying to gently set the bars down on the bedspread, but it was no use. They were too heavy. They slipped from her grasp and crashed onto the floor with a loud boom which shook the whole room.

Behind her a key turned in the lock. Nikki scrambled onto the rough stone ledge of the windowsill, one leg dangling over the side of the building. She gasped as she realized how high up she was. Three or four stories, at least. Way too high to jump. She heard the door open behind her. In desperation she looked over at the building across the way. Only a narrow alleyway separated the two buildings, but it was still too far to jump. Ten feet at least. But there was a wooden balcony on the story below, jutting out from the side of the other building. She'd have to jump outwards and let herself fall down to the balcony. Nikki pushed off from the windowsill as hard as she could, and then she was falling. In her terror the fall seem to last for hours.

The impact as her stomach hit the rail of the balcony knocked the wind out of her. For a minute all she could do was dangle there, half on the balcony, half off.

"Whatcha doing?"

"I think she's playing a game. Maybe she'll let us play too."

Nikki slowly lifted her head up, groaning as darts of pain shot up her spine. Two little kids, a girl and a boy about eight years old, were standing on the balcony staring at her. Nikki tried to speak but her squashed diaphragm wouldn't let her. Slowly she swung one leg and then the other over the side of the rail and collapsed onto the balcony.

"Who's that?" said the little girl, pointing upwards.

Nikki turned to find a black-cloaked Lurker staring down at her from the window she'd jumped from. She scrambled to her feet, holding her ribs and trying to catch her breath. "Playing hide and seek," she rasped. "Need to hide, fast."

The little girl nodded. "Come on. You can hide under my bed. Rupert is hiding under there, but he won't tell."

The little boy rolled his eyes. "She can't hide there, silly. That's the first place anyone looks when we play hide and seek. You always hide there and you always get caught." He put his hand over his mouth and leaned close to Nikki. "Rupert is her stuffed rabbit," he whispered. "I'm too old for baby things like stuffed rabbits. C'mon. I know where you can hide." He grabbed Nikki's hand and pulled.

Nikki let him lead her off the balcony into a room that was piled high with baskets full of laundry. In one corner a fireplace held coals burned down to glowing embers. An old-fashioned iron and ironing board were setup in front of the fire.

"Good thing Ma's downstairs having her tea," said the boy. "She don't like us playing in here, cause of the fire." He pulled Nikki over to a square hole in the wall opposite the fireplace. The hole was four feet above the floor and two feet square. It opened into blackness. The boy dumped a basket full of sheets off of a rickety chair and dragged the chair in front of the hole. He looked expectantly at Nikki as if the next step was obvious.

"Um," said Nikki, peering into the hole.

"Don't worry," said the boy, pushing at her impatiently. "My brother Tom uses it all the time when he's trying to get out of chores. And he's big. Bigger than you. He only got stuck once, and that's cause he had a chicken in his arms. He said the chicken was tired of just laying eggs and wanted a thrill. Anyway, once he let go of the chicken he got unstuck. Course, he landed on the chicken when he came out the other end of the chute. The chicken got killed, but I guess it had a thrill before it got squashed."

"But where does the chute go?" asked Nikki.

The boy rolled his eyes again. "Down to the laundry wagon, of course. You slide down and plop right into the wagon onto all the sheets and stuff. I do it all the time."

"You do not," said the little girl. "You're way too scared. Tom tried to put you in once and you cried louder than Mary." She leaned toward Nikki. "Mary's our baby sister. She's only one year old and she cries so loud it hurts my head."

"I don't cry," said the boy, punching his sister on the arm.

"Hey, none of that," said Nikki, climbing onto the chair and trying to ignore the pain in her ribs. She awkwardly pulled herself into the hole feet-first. "Do you know if the wagon's down there now? I'd much rather land in a pile of laundry than crash onto the cobblestones."

The boy reached up and patted her head. "Don't worry. Ma just sent a whole bunch of sheets down. She always fills the wagon right before her tea break."

Nikki nodded. "Okay. Well, thanks for your help. And don't hit your sister anymore." She closed her eyes and let go.

The chute was steeper than she'd expected and she found herself hurtling downward at an alarming rate. She tried to slow herself down by dragging her hands and feet on the sides of the chute but she couldn't get a grip on the waxed and polished wood. Just when she was sure her trip down was going to end in a broken neck she shot out of the end and landed with a thump on a bag full of laundry. The wagon she'd landed in was overflowing with bags full of sheets, dresses, and tablecloths. In one corner was a basket full of heavily embroidered velvet cloaks.

Nikki cautiously poked her head over the side of the wagon. It was parked in a quiet alley and there was a horse hitched to its front. Two men were sitting on wooden barrels near the horse, smoking pipes. Nikki quickly ducked back down and squirmed under a pile of laundry bags.

"Well, guess we should get a move on," said one of the men.

Nikki heard the horse stamp its hooves.

"Yeah, guess so. Even old Minerva wants to get going, don't you girl?"

The horse nickered and Nikki felt the wagon rock as the two men climbed aboard.

"So where's this load going to?"

"City Hall first. Got to deliver some of those fancy cloaks which her highness, Miss Fortuna the Most Annoying, likes to wear."

"Martha was complaining a blue streak this morning about them cloaks. She says the embroidery is a bear to get clean. She had to wash 'em three times. And she had a special order from some guest of Fortuna's which gave her no end of trouble. Apparently this Mr. Picky likes his sheets as spotless as a new lamb's first wool."

"Oh yeah, he's a stickler for cleanliness, so I've heard. Lots of rumors about him are flying round town. Set himself up in the King's rooms in City Hall he has. Though not many have noticed, seeing as how the King hasn't visited us here in good old D-ville in many a year. They say Fortuna visits Mr. Clean-and-Spotless in the King's chamber every night, though I have my doubts about that. Kinda old for that sort of thing, Fortuna is. I saw this mystery guest of hers yesterday. Crossing the main square with his nose in the air as if he was the King himself. Wanders around in black robes and leather sandals that never show the tiniest speck of dust, so they say. With his black robes and his lily-white skin he looks like he just woke up from a nap in a coffin."

Nikki gasped. Rufius was here in Deceptionville.

"What was that?" asked one of the men.

"What was what?"

"That noise. Sounded like somebody coughed."

"Probably just old Minerva. I gave her a bag of oats this morning. Makes her a bit wheezy."

Nikki heard the seat of the wagon creak, as if one of the men was leaning over it. She held her breath, but the wagon didn't stop and the men soon settled back into their conversation.

"Heard the news about the mayor?"

"Oh yeah, about how he's gone missing? Them rumors been flying for months now."

"Yeah, but there's new happenings. Seems his body was found."

"You don't say! Well, I don't mind admitting I thought the bloke was just off somewhere with one of his lady friends. He was always taking off to Muddled Manor to visit the Duchess, Lady Ursula. Spent more time at the Manor with her than he did in his office. And to think he was dead and gone this whole time."

"Looks like it. Martha heard about it from one of the kitchen workers at City Hall. Two of the city councilors personally saw his body. Was the mayor himself, dead as dust."

"Where'd they find him?"

"In the river."

"Drowned hisself?"

"Maybe. Nobody knows for sure. Maybe he was drunk and just fell in, but seems he had his skull bashed in."

"Could'a happened in the river. Maybe he just fell in and got knocked around on the rocks."

"Maybe, or maybe somebody helped him along by banging him on the head and then pushing him in the river."

"That's some pretty nasty business. Who'd a done such a thing?"

"My money's on this mystery guest of Fortuna's. He's creepy enough to go about bashing people on the head."

"Can't go around accusing people of murder just cause they look creepy. If that's the way the law worked we'd have to accuse half the people in the Wolf's Hide tavern."

"Ugh. Don't mention that place to me. Stopped in there for a pint once when I was just a lad, but never again. Lurker hangout, that place is."

"If you ask me, it's them blasted Lurkers who done in the mayor. Right up their alley, that kind of thing is."

"Probably right, you are. And I bet I know who paid 'em to do it. Miss Fortuna herself. She's been angling for the mayor's job for ages, ever since she arrived in town. Wants people bowing down to her and calling her Madame Mayor."

"Could'a been her, I guess. Or could'a been old Avaricious. He runs the Lurkers in this town."

"This town's goin' to the dogs, I says. The mayor was a worthless old coot, but he wasn't in the same league as Fortuna or Avaricious when it comes to underhanded doings. I say we give City Hall a wide berth from now on."

"Well, don't know about that. Martha gets a lot of business from the Hall. The washing of Fortuna's cloaks alone brings in half our rent money. And we got four kids to feed. Can't go around dropping clients just cause we don't like 'em."

"I suppose. Still, let's be as quick as we can. Drop off the cloaks and get out of there. I'll spot you a pint at the Market Tavern."

"You can spot me two pints. And a bowl of stew. I was up half the night helping Martha with the washing. Them wet sheets are darn heavy. I've worked me up a powerful appetite."

One of the men clicked his tongue and the horse nickered in response. Nikki felt the wagon speed up. She was rushing toward City Hall and Rufius whether she wanted to or not.

End of Book Three

Nikki's adventures in the Realm of Reason continue in the fourth book of the *Logic to the Rescue* series: *Mystics and Medicine.*

The Logic to the Rescue series

Logic to the Rescue
The Prince of Physics
The Bard of Biology
Mystics and Medicine
The Sorcerer of the Stars

The Hamsters Rule series

Hamsters Rule, Gerbils Drool
Hamsters Rule the School

Excerpt from Mystics and Medicine

Chapter One

S OMEBODY IN DECEPTIONVILLE was a bed-wetter. Nikki held her nose as she picked her way across the pile of wet sheets covering the stone floor. She was deep in the basement of City Hall, in the laundry room. The only light came from the embers glowing under cauldrons full of steaming water and wet sheets. A clanking sound came from somewhere in the distance, but no voices could be heard. The laundry workers had left for the day.

Nikki shivered. The room was probably hot and humid during the work day, but now that its fires were dying it was too cold for the silk tunic and jeans she had on. She squinted into the darkness. Surely somewhere in all these piles of laundry was something she could wear. One of Fortuna's heavy velvet cloaks would be just the thing. They'd been piled in a wicker basket in the laundry cart which had carried her to City Hall. The cart had dumped its bags and baskets down a chute in the wall and she'd slid down with them. The basket containing the cloaks had bounced off her head and rolled into a corner somewhere. She retraced her steps back to the chute. Her foot bumped into the basket before she saw it. She pulled out one of the heavy cloaks and threw it over her shoulders, then quickly snatched it off again. Thick swirls of embroidery covered the outside of the cloak.

There were even some hard lumps which felt like jewels. It was a very flashy item of clothing and people had undoubtedly seen Fortuna wearing it many times. If someone saw Nikki wearing it she'd get arrested for stealing. She felt around inside the cloak and up under its hood. The inside was smooth, thick wool. She turned the cloak inside out and put it back on. The jewels dug into her shoulders, but a few scratches were better than a cell in the City Hall dungeons.

As her eyes adjusted to the darkness she noticed the faint outline of stone steps leading up out of the basement. She carefully made her way toward them, her Nikes slipping on soapy puddles and what felt like sand. She knelt down and scooped up a pinch, rolling it between her fingers. A faint ammonia smell met her nose. It wasn't sand, it was lye, an ancient form of soap made by mixing animal fat with the potassium hydroxide derived from wood ash. The laundry probably used it on the bedsheets which were heaped all over the floor. Lye was too harsh to use on things like the cloak she was wearing. And it could also burn your skin. She rinsed her fingers in the puddle at her feet and cringed as she thought of the laundry workers who had to work with the lye every day, probably without gloves. From what she'd seen of the Realm worker safety was not exactly a high priority.

She pulled the hood of the cloak over her head and slowly climbed the stone steps, listening carefully. The clanking noise was getting louder, but she still couldn't hear any voices. After two stories the stairs opened into a circular room with wooden rafters stretching high overhead. Faint rays from the setting sun came through narrow slits cut in the thick stone walls. Nikki saw at once what was causing the clanking noise: a huge hammer was crashing down onto an anvil, banging down about once per second. She glanced quickly around the room. No workers were in sight. The hammer was hard at work all on its own.

She tiptoed over to it. The hammer was pounding down onto a long strip of grayish metal draped over the anvil. The handle of the hammer was lashed to a long wooden post stretching across the room. The other end of the post was being lifted up and down by a wooden shaft which rose up out of a dark gap in the floor. The sound of rushing water echoed from the gap. Nikki knelt down beside the gap and squinted down into the darkness. Sure enough, the waterwheel she'd been expecting to see was churning away in the depths. Deceptionville's City Hall was near the river. Part of the river must have been diverted into a channel underneath the building to power the waterwheel. The whole contraption was called a hammer mill. She'd seen a picture of one in her European history textbook back at Westlake High School. They'd been used in the Middle Ages to pound iron ore. One hammer mill could do the work of many blacksmiths. The shaft connected to the waterwheel converted the circular motion of the wheel to an up-and-down motion, just like the rotating crankshaft in a car engine moved the pistons up and down. The waterwheel could exert a lot more force than a man holding a hammer. And you didn't have to pay the waterwheel, which was good for the wheel's owner but probably put a lot of blacksmiths out of work.

The long strip of metal was also connected to the waterwheel by a system of gears. Nikki followed the snaking metal as it unrolled from a coil and scraped across the stone floor. As the strip was pulled across the anvil the hammer pounded out small disks of the gray metal. The finished disks slid off the anvil into a waiting basket. Nikki fished one out of the basket. Even in the dim light she could make out letters along its edge and a picture of something in the middle. It was obviously a coin. She was surprised to find that it bent easily. The metal was a very soft one, probably tin or lead. Strange metals to make coins out of. The only coins she'd seen so far in the Realm were gold and silver ones, but this disk couldn't possibly be made of silver. She wouldn't have been able to bend silver so easily. Silver was ranked as a 2.5 on the Mohs scale, which measured the hardness of metals. Tin and lead were only a 1.5 on the scale. Much softer than silver. And of course, less valuable. Nikki stared down at the coin in her hand. Was this just a new kind of coin, or had someone gotten the idea to make counterfeit money? A few likely counterfeiters leapt immediately to mind: Rufius, Fortuna, and Avaricious. She absent-mindedly felt the jewels sewn into the cloak she was wearing. The last time she'd seen Fortuna had been in the dungeon of the Confounded Castle in the Haunted Hills. The fortune teller had seemed desperate for money and had tried to force her to turn lead into gold. But now Fortuna was wearing cloaks decorated with jewels. She must have found a way to become rich. Counterfeiting was certainly one way to do that, as long as you weren't caught and thrown in jail.

Nikki tucked the coin into the pocket of her jeans. If she ever managed to find Fuzz and Athena again she'd show them the coin. They'd know what to do about it. But right now she had other problems. Like how to get out of City Hall without being caught by the Rounders. She looked around. Half-hidden by the waterwheel was an iron door she hadn't noticed before. It was partly ajar. She pulled the hood of her cloak farther down over her face and crept to the door, cautiously poking her head out. The door led into a long hallway decorated with tapestries and suits of armor. There was no one in sight, but she could hear voices and the clink of dishes coming from one end of the hall. Nikki took a deep breath and slid into the hallway, hugging the wall. She looked up and down. There was only one exit: toward the voices.

Sweat broke out on her forehead. She couldn't just walk into a room where it sounded like a large group of people were having dinner. Someone was sure to notice her. She was just about to slide back into the room with the hammer when she heard a man's voice coming from behind her.

"Get another basket, will ya?" said the voice. "This one's nearly full."

"Why don't we knock off for the day?" said another voice. "Me innards are so empty I could eat this here basket."

"Fortuna wants ten baskets sent to Kingston tonight and we've only got six. Yer innards'll just have to wait."

Nikki didn't wait to hear any more about the man's innards. She darted back into the hallway and headed toward the sound of clinking dishes. When she reached the end of the hall a tapestry of a deer surrounded by hunting dogs blocked the passageway. The deer had a desperate look on its face. Nikki gave it a little pat. She knew exactly how it felt. The tapestry was moving slightly, blown by air currents. Nikki knelt down and peered under its bottom edge, which was lined with tassels and dragging on the floor. She could see booted feet and the hems of ladies dresses. The feet were moving around more than she'd expected. Maybe they'd finished eating and were getting up from the table. They were conversing in loud voices. Her hopes rose. With all the movement and noise she might go unnoticed. She slowly pulled back one side of the tapestry and slid around it.

The room she found herself in was a large oak-paneled hall. It had an arched ceiling painted with fat angels lying on puffy pink clouds and grinning down at the people below. About a hundred people filled the room. Some sat at an immense oak dining table sipping wine and nibbling at cheese and grapes piled on silver platters. Others were milling around the room, chatting in small groups. There was a table loaded with dirty dishes against the wall near the tapestry door. Nikki quickly lifted the table's linen tablecloth and ducked underneath. She sat crossed-legged on the cold stone floor and peered out through a slit in the tablecloth. No one had noticed her, probably because most of them seemed extremely drunk. They were leaning on each other, sloshing the wine out of their goblets and laughing like hyenas. One lady, dressed very elegantly in a white satin gown with gold lace, spilled red wine down the front of her dress and just laughed and went on talking.

Nikki watched as waiters cleared plates and dirty wine goblets from the table and disappeared with them into a back room. At the other end of the hall was a raised platform surrounded by flags. Nikki recognized a purple flag with a golden crown in the middle. The same flag had flown on the ramparts of Castle Cogent, the residence of the King. She also recognized a forest-green flag with a circle of silver fish. She'd seen it flying on the tallest tower of the Southern Castle in Kingston. She'd also seen it on the roof of the mansion belonging to the Prince of Physics. She wondered if it was the Prince's flag or the flag of the city of Kingston. A cloaked figure stood in front of the flags. The figure's back was toward her, but it was wearing a cloak just like the one Nikki herself had on. Except the figure on the platform was wearing their cloak right-side out, with all its rich embroidery on display and its jewels glittering in the fading sunlight coming in from windows set high in the walls.

Fortuna. Nikki's eyes narrowed as she watched the fortune teller's grey-streaked hair sway across her humped back. Fortuna was talking to someone but Nikki couldn't see who it was. The person was seated and hidden from view by Fortuna's cloak. They seemed to be arguing about something. The fortune teller's arms were waving wildly in the air, her cloak flapping like the wings of a giant bird. Finally Fortuna threw up her arms in disgust and turned to face the room.

Nikki's hands clenched. Fortuna had been arguing with Rufius. He was seated in what looked like a throne. He had one leg thrown over its arm, his sandaled foot swinging lazily back and forth. His black tunic was as spotless as ever and his pale skin seemed to glow in the dim light of the hall.

Fortuna stepped to the edge of the platform and clapped her hands. The noise level lowered a bit, but it took a lot more clapping to get everyone to stop talking. Nikki grinned. Apparently the fortune teller didn't have quite as much authority as she felt she deserved.

"Quiet everyone," shouted Fortuna. "Let's settle down. I'm glad you're all enjoying the wine, which comes from my own vineyards in the Haunted Hills, but it's time to get down to business." She snapped her fingers at a waiter standing at the back of the platform. He darted behind a curtain and reappeared carrying a silver tray filled with small pots and glass bottles. Fortuna chose a midnight-blue ceramic pot from the tray and held it up.

"Lily of the Night," Fortuna announced dramatically. "The lotion in this little pot will make all blemishes vanish instantly. All age spots and wrinkles will disappear, never to be seen again. Ladies, one pot of this will make it look as if you've not yet reached your twenty-first birthday."

Several oohs and aahs sounded from the women in the room, with the woman in the wine-stained silk dress giving a loud shriek of joy, but Nikki also heard a few snorts of skepticism. One woman pointed at Fortuna's face and whispered something to her neighbor, who laughed. Nikki guessed she was pointing out that the wrinkles on Fortuna's face were so dark they looked like they'd been drawn on with charcoal. Apparently the fortune teller didn't use her own products, which made Nikki wonder exactly what was in them. She recognized the workmanship of the bottles on the tray. They'd obviously come from Avaricious's workshop. Knowing the low safety standards in his shop she had no doubt that the products Fortuna was selling contained lots of untested and probably harmful ingredients.

Fortuna ignored the skeptical snorts and put the pot back on the tray. She selected a round little bottle made of crimson glass and waved it above her head. Even the skeptic's eyes followed the little bottle as it glowed in the light of the candles which waiters were lighting in the hall.

"Panther's Pride!" proclaimed Fortuna. "Made from the thickest, richest hairs of the mighty jungle cats which roam the deepest reaches of the Southern Isles!" She uncorked the little bottle and gestured to a bald man in a purple velvet tunic who was standing in the middle of the crowd. He came forward uncertainly and twitched nervously when Fortuna poured a drop of silvery liquid onto his head. She rubbed it in vigorously. "Your head may be shiny as an egg right now, my friend, but just wait. Use this miraculous potion every day and you'll soon have the thickest head of hair imaginable. Every woman you meet will swoon at the sight of your youthful virility!"

A loud chuckle came from Rufius. Fortuna ignored him and placed the little bottle back on the tray. She dismissed the waiter and turned back to the crowd. "Friends! All of these wonderful items are now ready for sale. We are making them available to you, owners of the largest and most successful shops in Deceptionville. I guarantee that they'll generate huge profits for you. An entire room right here in City Hall is filled to the ceiling with cases of Lily of the Night, just waiting for your orders. We can ship cases anywhere in the Realm. For you, my very best of friends, I offer a discount of ten percent off the production cost. I'll actually lose money! This offer won't last long! If you'd like a chance to view our overflowing storerooms please follow me!"

Fortuna descended the steps on the side of the platform and sauntered from the hall, her cloak swaying behind her. A few of the guests turned back to their wine goblets, but most of them followed Fortuna. Soon only the waiters, a few drunken guests, and Rufius were left. Rufius sat humming to himself, swinging his foot and smiling at some private joke.

Nikki watched him. She guessed that the carved throne he was lounging in belonged to the King of the Realm. The laundry workers whose cart she'd hitched a ride in had been talking about the King's apartments in City Hall. They'd said that Rufius was living in the apartments. It looked like Rufius was trying to take the King's place here in Deceptionville, just like he'd tried to in Kingston. In Kingston he hadn't succeeded, not yet anyway, mainly due to the power and influence of the Prince of Physics. She guessed that Rufius might have more success here in Deceptionville, which was a corrupt place and not loyal to the King, or to anyone or anything other than money.

Rufius continued to sit there, humming to himself. Nikki was beginning to wonder if he was going to stay there all night when she heard ponderous footsteps approaching. Avaricious waddled into the hall, his purple robes swishing. The fat workshop owner waved a hand lazily at Rufius, the diamond rings on his sausage-like fingers sparkling in the candlelight.

"So it went well, I take it?" said Avaricious, pouring himself a goblet of wine. "The fish took the bait?"

Rufius sniggered. "Oh yes. They swallowed the bait and most of the fishing line. These potions of Fortuna's should add a nice bit of gold to the city's treasury."

Avaricious raised an eyebrow. "To the city's treasury? So the money will go straight to road repairs, schools, and orphanages?"

"Certainly," said Rufius with a grin. "And I believe the city needs a new bridge over the river as well. We mustn't forget the bridge. Of course, you'll get your cut before the roads, bridges, and orphans."

"I'd better," said Avaricious. "And the cut had better be a big one. My workshop put many hours into making all those potions."

"Using only the finest ingredients, I'm sure," said Rufius. "Tell me, who exactly did you test these potions on? I heard a rumor that all your alchemists threatened to quit if Panther's Pride got anywhere near their scalps."

Avaricious shrugged. "Any ill effects will show up when the first customers start using the potions. We can blame any rashes, bleeding or deaths on Fortuna. She's made herself the public face of the whole scheme, after all. The public will take any complaints they have to her. And I'm sure she'll be her usual kind and compassionate self."

Rufius laughed. "Come on. We'd better go check up on her. We can't afford to have her guests wandering all over the building."

Nikki waited until she couldn't hear their footsteps anymore and then cautiously poked her head out from under the tablecloth. The waiters had all gone into the back room. She could hear them washing the dishes. She glanced warily at the few remaining guests, but they were all so drunk they were nearly unconscious. She crawled out from under the table and tiptoed to the door of the hall.

A quick peek around the door showed that she was near the main entrance to the building. A vast lobby with stone columns two-stories high echoed faintly with the sound of Fortuna's voice off in the distance. The hall was on the second floor of the lobby. No one was in sight. Nikki darted to the stone parapet surrounding the lobby and looked down. The lobby's polished marble floor glistened in the light from torches mounted on the walls. A sudden cough echoed off the marble floor and Nikki jumped, looking wildly around. There was no one on her level. She cautiously leaned farther over the parapet. It was a guard. She hadn't spotted him before because his little wooden guard hut was tucked against the wall on the ground floor, right below her.

Very slowly she untied her Nikes and took them off. She knew from a school field trip to the state capital building in Wisconsin that rubber-soled shoes squeaked on marble floors. She looked around. Three corridors branched off from the level she was on, but she didn't know which to choose. Her plan had been to get out of City Hall as quickly as possible, but she couldn't just walk out past the guard. He probably knew most of the people who worked in the building. He was sure to stop her and ask her what she was doing there. She waited, listening hopefully for sounds of snoring from below her, but no such luck. The guard seemed to be wide awake at his post. He coughed, shuffled his feet, and hummed a tune under his breath.

There was no choice. The main entrance wasn't going to work. She'd have to find another way out. She chose a corridor at random and tiptoed to it in her stocking feet, breathing a sigh of relief when she was out of sight of the lobby.

The corridor seemed to stretch for miles. She had no idea that Deceptionville's City Hall was so enormous. She'd only had a brief glimpse of the exterior the last time she'd been in Deceptionville. She passed door after door as she went deeper into the building. Most of the rooms looked like offices, with scrolls and parchments piled on carved oak tables. There was a strong smell of candle wax, but no lights were burning in the rooms. All the workers had gone home for the day.

The cold marble floor of the corridor soon chilled her stocking feet. The room she was passing had a wooden bench just inside the door, so she ducked in and sat down to put her shoes back on. She had just finished tying her laces when a sudden movement caught her eye. She jumped up, stifling a gasp.

"It's all right, young lady. No need to be afraid. It's only me, old Geber."

Tucked away in a dark corner of the room was a very old man sitting in a chair. His long white beard reached nearly to his lap and his bald head shone in the moonlight coming in through a lead-paned window. He picked up the black cat which had been napping in his lap and place her gently on the floor. The cat hissed softly and stalked out of the room.

The old man chuckled. "Poor old Rowena. She's not getting any younger and she doesn't like having her sleep disturbed. I'm afraid you caught me having a bit of a snooze as well." He unhooked a cane dangling from the arm of the chair and slowly raised himself to his feet. "Would you like some tea, my dear?" Not waiting for an answer he hobbled over to a brick stove which had been built into the outer wall.

Nikki watched warily as he struck a piece of flint against a block of white quartz. Sparks flew into a small pile of straw nestled in a depression on the stove top. A flame soon grew and the old man added a few sticks of wood to the pile. He placed a three-legged iron trivet over the flame and put a tea kettle on top. "Hand me that pail of water, will you my dear?" he asked, pointing to a corner of the room.

Nikki glanced from the corner to the door of the room and back again. Should she run? If the old man started yelling the guard from the lobby would be up in a flash. Right now the old man was the only person who knew she was in the building. If he raised the alarm she'd have guards hunting all over the place for her. It seemed like a better idea to stay and keep him happy.

"Um, sure," she said, fetching the pail.

The old man took it from her and carefully poured water into the tea kettle. He handed the pail back. "Just put it out in the hall, please. One of the errand boys will refill it for me tomorrow morning."

Nikki took the pail out to the corridor. There was still no one in sight. She set the pail down on the floor, careful to make no noise. When she re-entered the room she saw that the old man had lit a torch on the wall. By its light she could see that the room was different from the others she'd passed. It was more laboratory than office. Glass beakers were piled on a work table and one wall held shelves stacked with glass jars full of colored powders. It reminded her of Gwen's laboratory in the basement of Muddled Manor.

"Just shut the door, will you my dear?" said the old man as he spooned tea leaves into two mugs. "Don't want that blasted Thomas up here. He's the night guard. He gets bored and likes to leave his post whenever he hears me pottering about. He drinks my tea and brags for hours about his success at dice games and his winnings at cards. Drives me mad. One of these days I swear by all the ghosts in the Haunted Hills that I'm going to poison him just so I can have some peace and quiet. And don't think that I wouldn't get away with it. Oh, I'd get away with it all right, just like that conniving young whippersnapper Rufian got away with poisoning old Mally. Not that anyone misses old Mally, of course. Likely even the King is glad he's gone. Never very popular, was old Mally."

Nikki quietly shut the heavy oak door. She doubted that the old man was dangerous. He moved so slowly, hobbling on his cane, that she was sure she could be out the door and far down the corridor before he had moved two steps. "Who's Mally?" she asked.

"The King's advisor," said the old man. "Well, he used to be the King's advisor. Dead now, as I said, and not missed. His real name was Maleficious, though I always called him Mally. We were at school together. Everyone called him Mally there. Maleficious was a ridiculous, pompous name for a little boy. And he grew up to be a ridiculous, pompous old fool."

Nikki sat down on a high wooden stool next to the workbench. "So, you think someone poisoned him, sir?"

"Call me Geber," said the old man. "Everyone does. I don't mind. I don't stand on ceremony. Sometimes they call me Mr. Geber, but *that* I do mind. Means they want something." He shuffled to the workbench, his cane hooked on his forearm, the two mugs of tea sloshing in his shaking hands.

Nikki hopped off her stool and took the mugs, setting them on the workbench.

Geber slowly lowered himself onto a stool. "Can't prove poison," he said, stirring his tea with an ink-stained quill from the workbench. "It's just my little hunch. Mally was an old man. He hadn't left Castle Cogent in years, and he died in his chambers in the castle. His death could have been due to natural causes. But I still have some old acquaintances up at the castle. People right in the inner circle of the King. They all say Mally had severe stomach cramps and vomited blood right before he died. Arsenic poisoning would be my guess. There are deposits of arsenic in caves in the Haunted Hills. People mine the deposits to use as rat poison. Pretty easy to get your hands on it. I have some of it here." He waved a hand at the shelves on the wall.

Nikki glanced uneasily at the jars on the shelves. She stared down at her mug of tea then pushed it away without taking a sip. "So, if he was poisoned, who do you think did it?" she asked.

"Rufian," said Geber, nodding his head decisively. "You mark my words, young lady. It was Rufian. Snivelling, conniving little son of a cheese-monger. He was here in D-ville when Mally died, but that doesn't mean anything. Probably bribed one of the castle servants to slip the poison into Mally's wine."

"Do you mean Rufius?" asked Nikki.

"Of course," said Geber. "Rufius the Rufian. I just call him Rufian for short. Call him that to his face, I do. He hates it. Makes him turn purple, which is highly amusing, let me tell you."

"That seems like dangerous thing to do," said Nikki. "Making Rufius mad, I mean. He's become quite powerful as far as I can tell. And he's got powerful friends, like Avaricious and the Knights of the Iron Fist."

Geber shrugged and took a swig of tea. "When you're as old as I am you don't care as much about making enemies. I suppose Rufian could have me poisoned, same as he did Mally, but so what? I'm only good for another year or two at the most anyway. Little Rufian. Oh, I have his number. He wants power. And money, but mostly power. I've met his kind before. He likes to give orders, likes to be important, likes people bowing down to him. He used to bring cheese from his parent's shop in Popularnum up to the kitchens at Castle Cogent. But he didn't confine himself to the kitchens. Oh no, not he. He chatted up every courtier in the place and took to flattering old Mally. Soon as you can blink he was Mally's apprentice. Wormed his way into the King's good graces as well. And now little Rufian has set himself up in the King's apartments here in City Hall."

"Did you know that Fortuna the Fortunate is also here?" said Nikki. "She's selling creams and potions to shopkeepers from all over the Realm. They just had a big meeting downstairs. She's showing them her storerooms full of potions right now."

Geber didn't answer. Instead he creakily raised himself from his stool and tottered over to a shelf on the wall. He picked up a little clay pot and carried it back to the workbench. "Lily of the Night," he said.

Nikki stared at it. "Where did you get it? Did you make it?"

"Of course not," said Geber indignantly. "Those two-bit hacks over at Avaricious's workshop made it. I had one of my errand boys steal me a sample so I could have a look at it. Find out what's in it."

"And did you find out?"

Geber nodded. "Oh yes. It wasn't hard. I took a bit out of this pot and heated it over an open flame. It was animal fat, mostly. Pig fat, probably from the pig farms near Kingston. To mask the smell they added bits of lavender. No need of tests for that, you can smell it with your own nose. After I melted off the fat there was a small amount of grayish powder left. I had my suspicions about that, so I mixed the powder with some vinegar."

"You were testing for lead," said Nikki. She had done something similar in her high school chemistry class, mixing a small piece of lead with vinegar and hydrogen peroxide to produce a white powder called lead acetate. Of course, in her chemistry class they'd worn gloves, aprons and safety goggles, and used lots of ventilation. And they'd disposed of the lead acetate in a hazardous waste container. She very much doubted that Avaricious's workshop was so cautious when they created Lily of the Night.

Geber raised his bushy white eyebrows. "That's right, young lady. How did you know that?"

"It was just a guess," said Nikki. "Lead used to be used in face powder. It turns the skin white. Some ladies like that, but it's very dangerous. Lead is poisonous." She poked at the gunk in the little pot with a piece of quill. "Is there enough lead in one pot of Lily of the Night to be dangerous?"

Geber stroked his long white beard. "No, not in one pot. But if a lady used say, a pot a week, well then problems would definitely arise. She could look forward to baldness, muscle spasms, mental problems, and even death."

Nikki stared down at the little pot. "We have to tell people."

Geber harrumphed. "Do our civic duty, you mean? Save the citizens of the Realm from themselves? Not an easy task, young lady. Don't really see how we can spread the word. And even if we could, many ladies of the Realm would ignore our warnings and keep slapping on Lily of the Night. Vanity is a powerful opponent."

"It's not just the ladies who are in danger," said Nikki. "Fortuna is also selling something called Panther's Pride, which is supposed to cure baldness in men. I bet it has a few dangerous ingredients as well."

Geber shrugged. "The male of the species is just as vain as the female. I suggest you drop the matter, my dear. You won't get far trying to save people from themselves."

"Maybe not, but I think we should at least try," said Nikki. "We might be able to convince a few people that Fortuna is selling dangerous products. We could do some kind of demonstration here in Deceptionville," said Nikki. "In the main square."

Geber shook his head. "We'd be thrown in the City Hall dungeons, young lady. Before we could get one word out. I've lived in D-ville most of my life. It's always been a corrupt place, with the Rounders and the city council taking bribes right and left. But things have become much worse lately. Rufian, Avaricious, and Fortuna have been running D-ville as if it was their own private kingdom. Fat old Avaricious has always been the town's biggest crook, but after he teamed up with Rufian and Fortuna the three of them took complete control of the city council. After the mayor was found dead the council announced that all large gatherings were now illegal. No parades, no speeches, and definitely no demonstrations. And besides, your idea of a demonstration won't work. There's no way to demonstrate the dangers of lead. Not in a quick public show. Lead is a slow poison. The effects don't show up for months, even years."

"But *you* know it's dangerous," said Nikki. "I'm a little surprised by that. I didn't think anyone in the Realm knew. I met a man in Avaricious's workshop who said he'd mixed lead glazes for pottery since he was a child. He said it was harmless, though it was obvious that he had severe mental problems, and the skin on both his arms was an ugly grayish-white."

Geber snorted. "I'm far from the only person in the Realm to know of lead's dangers. All of the alchemists in Avaricious's workshop know lead is poisonous. They're very careful not to handle it themselves. They get fools like the man you met to do the dangerous work of mixing lead compounds."

"All the more reason to tell the public . . ." Nikki began.

Geber waved an impatient hand. "Sorry young lady, but I'll have nothing to do with it. A fool's errand it is. No one will listen to you and you'll just get yourself in trouble. Now, this has been a lovely chat. It's nice to have some company other than my cat, but I think it's time for another little nap." He heaved himself off the stool and tottered back to the dark corner where he'd been dozing. Snores soon echoed around the room.

Nikki sat staring uncertainly at the little pot of Lily of the Night. As she was mulling over what to do an insistent meow came from out in the hall. She hopped off the stool and opened the room's heavy oak door. Rowena, Geber's black cat, strolled in and rubbed herself on Nikki's ankles.

Nikki scratched the cat under the chin, earning a cascade of purrs. "I have a cat, you know," she said to Rowena. "Well, she's still more of a kitten. Her name's Cation." Nikki sighed. She hoped Cation was okay. Fuzz wasn't fond of the kitten, but surely Athena or Gwen would look after her. She wondered where everyone in their little group was. Their last plan had been for Linnea lead them by secret trails to Kingston, and then to meet up with Griff's ship. Would they stick to that plan, or would they abandon it to search for her? She wasn't sure. She knew Fuzz and Athena felt responsible for her, since they'd taken her out of her own world and brought her to the Realm of Reason. Still, very bad things were happening in the Realm right now. Rufius and the Knights of the Iron Fist were trying to seize power from the King, and imps all over the Realm were being harassed and even attacked. Fuzz and Athena might feel they couldn't put their plans on hold. After all, they had no idea where she was. It could take them weeks to find her. It might be easier for *her* to find *them*. She knew where they were heading – Kingston harbor. But the idea of trying to get from Deceptionville to Kingston all by herself was scary. Just thinking about it made her feel tired. Geber's laboratory suddenly seemed much more appealing than wandering the dark corridors of City Hall. There was a cot against one wall, covered with wool blankets. Nikki stumbled over to it, yawning. She crawled under the blankets. Rowena jumped up on the cot and curled up next to her head and purred softly. Nikki was soon fast asleep.

Chapter Two

"**H**EY! YOU! WAKE Up. What're ya doin' in me kip?"

"Wha . . . ?" Nikki groggily poked her head out from under the woolen blanket. A boy about twelve years old was standing over her, looking distinctly annoyed. He was dressed in a rough linen shirt and pants and his bare feet were filthy. He reminded her of Curio. He had the same uncared for and un-parented look.

"Me kip," repeated the boy. "It's where I take me snoozes. You're in it." He kicked a leg of the cot for emphasis.

"Oh, sorry," said Nikki, clambering off the cot. "I didn't know."

"Don't mind him, young lady," said Geber, tottering toward them on his cane. "He's more bark than bite. And even his bark is more puppy than wolf."

The boy glared at him. "I'm plenty wolf," he said. "The blokes at the Wolf's Hide Tavern all say so. They wouldn't let me in if I weren't tough." He put his hands on his hips and puffed out his chest.

Nikki stifled the urge to laugh.

Geber waved his cane at the boy. "I've told you a hundred times, my boy. Stay away from that blasted place. Lurker hangout. That's what it is. You'll get yourself into more trouble than you can handle. Now go fetch some water for our morning tea."

The boy made a rude hand gesture and stalked out of the room.

Geber sighed. "He's not a bad boy, really. Just rough around the edges. No manners, because he had no parents to teach him any. His name is Sander. He was a pedestal baby. And like most of them he's unschooled and ill-mannered. Not their fault, of course."

"No, of course not," said Nikki, suddenly feeling less annoyed with the boy's rudeness. Curio had also been a pedestal baby. His mother had abandoned him on a stone pedestal which was somewhere in Deceptionville. She didn't know exactly where. Apparently this pedestal was used as a drop-off spot for orphans and unwanted children. Kind of like the way people would sometimes leave unwanted children at the hospital or the fire station back in her hometown in Wisconsin.

She felt a sudden longing to see her own mother. She'd been in the Realm of Reason for nearly two months now. It was very interesting and she'd made many new friends, but the flashes of homesickness were difficult to fight off sometimes. In the back of her mind lurked the horrifying thought that maybe the portal back to her own world was closed now. Maybe she was trapped here in the Realm forever. Sweat broke out on her forehead and she missed what Geber was saying to her.

"Pardon?" asked Nikki.

"I asked, young lady, whether you are staying for breakfast?" said Geber as he tottered over to the brick stove. "Our repasts aren't fancy, but we have plenty to share."

"Um, sure. Thank you very much," said Nikki, yawning and squinting at the sunlight streaming in from the window slits in the room's outer wall. She hadn't expected to sleep all night and she felt a bit disoriented. And she was still uncertain what to do about Fortuna and her dangerous, lead-laced potions.

"Just fetch a loaf of rye down if will be so kind," said Geber, waving his cane at a cupboard nailed to the wall above Nikki's head. "We keep the bread up there so the rats don't get at it, but I find it difficult to reach that high nowadays."

"Sure," said Nikki. She stretched on her tiptoes and was just able to reach the cupboard. She grabbed a fragrant loaf of dark rye bread and handed it to Geber, trying hard not to think about the rats that might have been scampering around her cot while she slept.

Geber sawed the loaf into thick slices and toasted them over an open flame on top of the brick stove. He handed a slice to Nikki. "There's butter in that little red pot on my workbench," he said. "No, wait. That's a salve I mixed for one of the blacksmiths in the market. He gets the most awful skin rashes." He peered nearsightedly around the room. "Now where did I put the butter?"

"It's over on da windowsill," said Sander, returning with a pail full of water. "I put it there meself so you wouldn't use it in one of yer potions." He poured water from his pail into an iron tea kettle on the stove and then fetched the butter, plunking it down on the workbench in front of Nikki. "She's not gonna eat all our bread, is she?" he asked, hungrily eyeing the toast Nikki was nibbling on.

"There's plenty to go around," said Geber, handing the boy a piece of toast. "You'll have to excuse Sander, young lady. He doesn't like sharing his food. Not that you can really blame him. Before I made him my assistant he was roaming the streets of D-ville scrounging for scraps in the garbage heaps."

Sander gobbled down his toast, scattering crumbs everywhere. Rowena slinked up to him and wound herself around his legs, mewling for handouts. Sander gave her a rough nudge with his foot.

"Now, now," said Geber. "No need for that, my boy. Rowena's just hungry, same as you." He offered a small piece of toast to the cat and she disappeared with it under the cot Nikki had slept on. "So, young lady," said Geber, "What are you up to today? Sander and myself will be down in the basement most of the day, making paper. You are most welcome to stay here, if you wish."

Nikki quickly swallowed the last bite of her toast. "Paper?" she asked in surprise. "I thought everyone here wrote on parchment."

Geber nodded. "Yes, parchment is the usual choice. It's durable and holds ink well. But it's expensive and only available after a cow or sheep has been killed. And the tanning process which makes the cowhide usable is very lengthy, not to mention smelly and unpleasant. Because of its expense parchment is only available to the upper classes. Consequently they are the only ones who can read and write. The farmers, field hands, fishermen and other laborers are mainly illiterate and uneducated. It makes them easy marks for wicked and power-hungry people such as Fortuna and Rufian." He paused to pour boiling water from the whistling tea kettle into three cups. He handed one to Nikki and joined her at the workbench. "Where was I? Oh yes. Paper. You see, one day last spring I happened to be browsing in the shop belonging to Avaricious. A large party of traders from the Southern Isles had just come into town and Avaricious was buying up all their wares. Among their spices and silks they had something I'd heard of but never seen with my own eyes. Paper they called it. Little squares of very light material. Useful, they said for writing upon. They refused to tell me the secret of how it was made, but I could tell simply by its feel and smell that it was made at least partly from wood."

"Spruce and pine," grunted Sander, slathering butter on another piece of toast.

Geber chuckled. "Yes, Sander is now very familiar with papermaking, aren't you, my boy?"

"Familiar with the rough parts," muttered Sander.

Geber clapped him on the back with an age-spotted hand. "Well, that's why you are in my employ, young sir. Because of your strong young back." He turned back to Nikki. "We have a machine down in the basement, one of my own design I humbly admit. It is connected to a waterwheel and it does the most difficult work, that of sawing the pine boards into small pieces. Of course, the logs must be loaded onto the machine in the first place, and I'm afraid that kind of heavy work is quite beyond me. Sander and a few of the other errand boys load the logs onto the sawing platform. After the sawing process another attachment to the waterwheel then pounds the small pieces of wood into pulp, but there are still many steps after that which must be done by hand."

Nikki sipped her tea and wondered about the waterwheel contraption she'd seen last night down near the laundry room. She was tempted to ask Geber if he'd designed it, but decided that might not be a good idea. If the coins it was busily banging out were counterfeit, as she suspected, then Geber must be part of the counterfeit scheme. He seemed like a nice old man, and she didn't want to believe he could be part of a crime like counterfeiting, but it was possible. She didn't know anything about him other than that he was an alchemist. An official one, apparently, since his laboratory was right inside of City Hall. But, a nice person or not, Geber might be useful. His papermaking had given her an idea.

End of Excerpt

Excerpt from Hamsters Rule, Gerbils Drool

Chapter One

M ELVIN STIRRED UNEASILY in his pile of sawdust shavings. The snuffly snores coming from the twin bed across the room were disturbing his rest. He crawled out of his nest and trundled down an orange plastic tunnel to a distant corner of his Hamster Habitat. Diving head first into a pile of cedar chips, he squirmed until only his chubby rear-end was visible. He twitched for a few seconds then settled back into sleep.

Melvin should have counted himself lucky. The snores of his owner, Miss Sally Jane Hesslop, who was eleven years old as of last Tuesday, were much quieter than usual due to Sally's head being buried under her Xena Warrior Princess bedspread. All that could be seen of Sally was a long strand of blonde hair with a wad of pink bubble gum stuck on the end of it.

The morning sun finished clearing the fog from San Francisco bay and lit up Sally's bedroom window. The light revealed quite a mess: Legos, comic books, sneakers, mismatched socks and a spilled can of Hungry Hamster Snacks were scattered across the floor. Sally was a firm believer in keeping all of her belongings in plain view. In an emergency (and most mornings were an emergency, as Sally had a talent for being late for school) precious time could be saved by getting dressed from the clothes on the floor.

This morning Sally's peaceful slumber was destined to last only a few more brief moments, for Robbie was out of bed and on the loose.

Robbie was Sally's four-year-old brother. He was famous up and down their neighborhood for his ability to eat anything dirt-related. Mud, clay, sand, litter box filler, anything lurking in the bottom of a flowerpot or fish tank, all were fair game. When it came to dirt Robbie was an omnivore. Though, of course, he had his favorites. The light fluffiness at the heart of the vacuum cleaner bag, the tasty compost at the roots of his grandmother's roses – these were special treats for special occasions, to be savored slowly and washed down with a good quality grape Kool Aid.

Today Robbie was up at his usual time of six a.m. He tiptoed into Sally's room, a stealthy menace in his footie pajamas and bike helmet. This helmet was a permanent item in Robbie's wardrobe. Robbie was fond of banging his head on things in a rhythmic pattern similar to certain popular hip-hop songs, so his father had started putting a helmet on him as soon as Robbie got out of bed.

Giggling softly and wielding a large rubber spatula, Robbie crept up to the snoring Sally. He pulled back the edge of the bedspread with one chubby fist and brought the spatula down with a satisfying thwhack on top of Sally's head.

"Aaaah!" Sally bolted upright, her scrawny arms swinging wildly as she tried to ward off her assailant. Her oversized Xena T-shirt billowed out, making her eighty-pound frame look twice its size. A neon-yellow post-it note which was stuck to her forehead fluttered in the breeze as she whipped around and grabbed the spatula from a chortling Robbie. Sally rained down a barrage of blows with the spatula onto Robbie's bike helmet. Robbie made a dash for the door, knocking over a stack of comic books. He was almost to safety, inches from escape, when he miscalculated the distance between the door jamb and his head. He bounced backwards off the door, his helmet taking most of the punishment, tripped over a half-built castle made of Legos, and toppled over onto the carpet with his feet in the air.

Sally leapt out of bed with a wild war cry and rained rubbery blows down on Robbie as if beating a stubborn batch of dough.

"Sally Jane, are you out of bed yet?" The voice floating in from the hallway sounded in desperate need of coffee. Sally's father's dearest dream was to sleep in past six a.m., a dream which was destroyed on a daily basis by Robbie and his spatula. Robbie had assigned himself the task of family alarm clock and he took his job seriously. If the first whack on the head didn't wake his target at six on the dot then Robbie would tirelessly whack until he got results. Mr. Hesslop had tried hiding the spatula in the back of the cereal cupboard, but Robbie had just switched to whacking with the toilet brush. Mr. Hesslop had quickly decided that he preferred the spatula, the toilet brush tending to catch in his hair.

Sally gave Robbie one final blow then grabbed his pajama feet and dragged him out of her room. "I'm up, Dad. I'm up," she shouted, leaving Robbie lying on his back in the hallway. Sally darted back into her room and slammed the door. She yawned, scratched her ear with the captured spatula, and surveyed her wardrobe. Her favorite pair of jeans, only slightly muddy around the knees, hung off the end of her bed. She pulled them on and selected a pink T-shirt from a pile under the window. As she pulled it over her head the post-it which was stuck to her forehead fluttered to the floor. Sally scooped it up and read it aloud.

"Charlie Sanderson must pay. Skedyul revenge for recess."

Sally's blue eyes narrowed to slits, and she smacked her palm with the spatula.

"Right. It's payday, Charlie. Today, after third period."

"OKAY, ROBBIE. YOU'VE had enough. Come and drink your juice."

Robbie, crouching over a scraggly fern which an aunt had given them for Christmas, ignored his Dad. He reached into the depths of the flowerpot and pulled up a fistful of loamy soil. He carefully picked off a ladybug which was crawling toward his thumb and then crammed the dirt into his mouth.

Mr. Hesslop sighed. He grabbed Robbie off the floor and plopped him into a chair at the kitchen table. Mr. Hesslop was a taller version of Sally Jane. Both father and daughter had dishwater blond hair, blue eyes, long skinny arms and legs, and pointy elbows. Short, chubby Robbie, with his dark hair and brown eyes, looked completely unrelated to his Dad and his eleven-year-old sister, a fact which Sally mercilessly exploited. She had convinced Robbie that he was on loan from the bank that their Dad worked at, and that he could be returned at any time if she just said the word. Robbie had responded to this threat by reducing Sally's spatula wake-up calls to once a week. His Dad still got the seven-day-a-week treatment though, Robbie guessing correctly that his Dad loved him too much to pack him up and store him in a bank vault.

"Robbie, you've got to stop eating dirt." Mr. Hesslop grabbed a paper napkin and wiped Robbie's muddy mouth. "Remember what Dr. Tompkins told you? If you don't stop you're going to have a tree growing in there." He tickled Robbie's stomach.

Robbie giggled. "Tree in tummy."

Sally wandered into the kitchen, bumping into the refrigerator. Her long, straight hair hung in front of her face like a curtain. She had attempted to braid pieces of it, and the attempt had not gone well. One braid sprouted from the top of her head like an overgrown onion. Another looked like it was growing straight out of her ear. She sat down at the kitchen table, one hand tangled in the rest of her unbraided hair, the other grabbing for a box of Cheerios.

Mr. Hesslop passed her the milk. "Sally Jane, why don't you let me help you with your hair? I'll make you look real pretty."

What could be seen of Sally's face under her hair looked suspiciously like it was rolling its eyes. "Daaad. I'm not trying to look pretty. I'm doing Xena braids. See, if you're in a fight you don't want your hair in your face. You can't see good."

"What fight?" Mr. Hesslop said sharply, his thin nose pointed at his daughter like a fox on the scent.

Sally smiled innocently. "I was just being hypometical, Dad. Sheesh."

"Hypothetical," said Mr. Hesslop. "Robbie, don't do that." He grabbed Robbie's juice glass, which was now half empty. Robbie had poured the rest onto the floor and was straining against his father's arm, eager to get down from the table to study (and taste) the effects of orange juice on dirty linoleum at close range.

Melvin waddled into the kitchen, his fluffy orange fur dusting a path along the un-swept floor, his nose twitching for food. He disappeared under Sally's chair, dodged her swinging feet, and settled in front of the puddle of orange juice. His tiny pink tongue darted out and lapped at lightning speed, aware that even Mr. Hesslop with his lazy housekeeping skills was unlikely to leave a bonanza like this lying around for long.

Fortunately for Melvin, Mr. Hesslop was distracted by the sound of a knock at the front door. He set Robbie down and went to greet their visitor. A few seconds later he reappeared with Darlene Trock-worthy, their next-door neighbor. A peroxide blond with heavy blue eye-shadow, a too-tight dress and too-high heels, Darlene occasionally babysat Robbie and Sally. Darlene and Robbie were best friends, mainly because Darlene let Robbie eat as much dirt as he wanted, but between Darlene and Sally it had been war from the start.

Darlene slid into a seat at the kitchen table, aiming a kick at Melvin on the way. "Is that rat loose again?" she asked, her mouth full of the toast she had grabbed off of Robbie's plate.

Sally glared at her. "He's not a rat, you dingbat."

"Sally, watch your manners," Mr. Hesslop said sharply.

"Bill, the kid's rhyming again. I thought you said she'd grow out of that." Darlene pouted at Mr. Hesslop, her bright red lipstick spattered with toast crumbs. The whole neighborhood knew that Darlene had her "sights set" on Bill Hesslop, but so far he had resisted her advances.

"She'll grow out of it eventually," said Mr. Hesslop. "It's just a phase. Robbie, don't do that."

Robbie had climbed off his chair and was sitting on the floor, rubbing Cheerios in the dust on the floor before eating them.

Mr. Hesslop picked him up. "I'll clean up Mr. Dirt Devil here and drop him at his preschool. Can you take Sally?"

The look Darlene shot Sally clearly said that she'd like to dump Sally in San Francisco bay. Darlene sighed heavily. "Yeah, sure." She pointed a warning finger at Sally, a long red fingernail raking the air like a claw. "But no rhyming, kid. I mean it. One Iambic what-ya-ma-callit and I'm selling you to the slave traders. They'll ship you to Nebraska and make you shuck corn 'til you're eighty."

Sally smiled at her sweetly. "Your wish is my command. And your head is filled with sand." Sally scooped Melvin up, put him on her shoulder, and marched out of the kitchen.

"Put that rat back in his cage." Darlene yelled after her. "And if you're not ready in ten minutes I'm leaving without you."

Chapter Two

———◗●◖———

SALLY AND DARLENE maintained a careful no-touching distance as they headed down the hill to Sally's school. When a bike rider on the sidewalk forced them to shrink the gap between them they automatically sprang apart again after the bike had passed, as if repelled by a magnetic field.

Darlene examined her makeup in a compact mirror as she tee-tered along, causing oncoming pedestrians to grumble as they jumped out of her way. Sally practiced karate kicks, viciously attacking the most dangerous looking trash cans and mailboxes along their route, her backpack flopping wildly on her shoulders.

Halfway down the hill a posse of poodles suddenly rushed out the front door of a tall apartment building and made straight for Sally. Sally threw herself down on her knees and scooped up the scruffy little white poodle which was leading the pack. The little poodle yapped excitedly, licking Sally's face. The other three poodles were tall, black, and dignified, with the fur on their heads shaped into elegant topknots. They sniffed at Sally's backpack and at Darlene's shoes. One of them lifted his leg and took aim at Darlene's stiletto. Darlene shrieked and jumped back.

"Brutus! No!"

A chubby little girl about Sally's age ran up to them and grabbed the peeing poodle. She had black curly hair and large dark eyes. She was wearing a plaid skirt, a starched white blouse, and black patent leather shoes which looked extremely uncomfortable. "Brutus, you bad dog! Sorry, Miss Trockworthy. My Mom's trying to train him not to pee on everyone, but he forgets sometimes." She herded the poodles back up the front steps of the apartment building. "C'mon Brutus, Caesar, Nero, and Fluffy. You can't come to school with us. Poodles are not allowed. Go back upstairs."

Sally waved goodbye to Fluffy and stood up, dusting off her knees. "Hi, Katie! Are you ready to rumble?"

The chubby girl looked at her in confusion. "Huh?"

Sally skipped around Katie, chanting. "Charlie's a boy, so he's not too bright. We'll shout with joy when we win this fight."

Katie picked up the book bag she had dropped during the poodle roundup. A worried frown crinkled her pale forehead. "I don't know, Sally. Remember what happened the last time you got into a fight at school? Billy Lauder's tooth got knocked out and Arnold the Iguana ate it and had to go to the Pet Hospital. I don't want Arnold to go to the Pet Hospital. He doesn't like it there. Remember the time I put my Mom's Lilac Mist hand lotion on him because he looked dry? I thought it would make him feel better, but it turned him all pink and he had to go to the Pet Hospital so they could make him green again. Arnold hates being pink. Pink is a girl's color, and Arnold's a boy iguana. Mr. Zukas says so. So you shouldn't fight."

Katie looked ready to cry. Her large eyes grew red-rimmed and shiny. Sally patted her on the shoulder and handed her a wadded up Kleenex which she pulled out of her backpack. She resumed skipping in circles.

"Arnold's not going to the Pet Hospital this time," said Sally. "I have a new Secret Revenge Plan, and there aren't any iguanas in the plan."

Katie sniffed and wiped her nose. She followed Sally and Darlene as they continued down the hill. "Oh. Well, I guess it's okay then. I'm glad Arnold isn't in your new Secret Revenge Plan, 'cause iguanas don't like fighting. They're pacifiers."

Sally stopped skipping and nodded knowingly. "Iguanas are pacifiers cause they can't do karate kicks." She demonstrated a karate kick, narrowly missing the nose of a passing Pomeranian. The Pomeranian growled at her and Sally growled back.

They reached the bottom of the hill and turned onto a narrow side street lined with gingko trees. The sidewalk was covered with fan-shaped gingko leaves. Sally swooshed at them with the toes of her sneakers, sending the leaves swirling like tiny doves. Katie carefully stepped on the bare patches of sidewalk, keeping her shiny patent leather shoes free of leaf mush. Up ahead the street was jammed with cars disgorging kids with backpacks. The kids ran into the fenced-in playground of Montgomery Elementary School, a three-story brick building with sturdy granite columns flanking its front door. The building had a basketball court on one side and a cluster of crooked pine trees on the other side.

"Okay, you two," said Darlene, finally closing her compact. "Get lost. One of your parents will pick you up after school. Don't know which parent. Don't care." She sauntered off, popping a wad of gum into her mouth. Sally stuck her tongue out at Darlene's retreating back.

"You shouldn't do that," said Katie, gasping in horror. "My Mom says that kids should always show adults the proper respect."

Sally snorted. "Darlene's not an adult. She's a doofus." She skipped around Katie, chanting. "Darlene, Darlene, she's not too keen. She's the biggest dunce you've ever seen."

Katie turned red. She quickly looked around to make sure that Darlene hadn't heard. Darlene was examining her nails as she walked away, completely oblivious to the kids dodging around her on the sidewalk. Katie breathed a sigh of relief and followed Sally into the school building.

"Okay, everyone settle down!" Mr. Zukas' deep voice boomed over the chaos in his fifth-grade classroom. He gave his sweater vest a firm tug and strode to the front of the class. "Get to your desks, pronto. Tommy, get your foot out of Kyle's mouth. Patricia, give Tiffany back her shoes. They're too small for you anyway, you clodhopper."

Thirty kids rushed to their seats with a sound like elephants tap dancing. Sally threw herself into her assigned seat in the front row of desks. Katie lowered herself demurely into the seat directly behind Sally. Arnold the Iguana calmly surveyed the classroom from his cage at the back.

Mr. Zukas opened a fat textbook. As he slowly searched for the page he wanted Sally started to fidget. She squirmed like an eel, sat on her hands, and finally couldn't contain herself any longer. She raised her arm and began waving it furiously back and forth. Mr. Zukas ignored her and turned another page.

Never one to be discouraged, Sally climbed onto her chair and waved both arms wildly like a pint-sized airport worker guiding a jumbo jet into a parking space.

"Sally Jane Hesslop," sighed Mr. Zukas, not looking up, "get down off of there before you break your neck. Not that I would mind, but the principal gets grumpy when students kick the bucket."

"Sorry, Mr. Zukas," said Sally, climbing down. "I just had a question. Can we have more discusses on evolution? Cause I looked it up on Google and a Google person says we came from tadpoles. I think it would be cool to be a tadpole. I had a tadpole once. I kept it in a Sprite bottle. After I drank the Sprite, of course. But then my brother Robbie drank the tadpole. Are we having fish sticks for lunch today?"

Mr. Zukas rubbed his forehead, looked longingly at the clock, and sighed again. "I haven't checked the lunch menu today, Sally. It's posted on the cafeteria door. You can check at recess. And no, we don't come from tadpoles. We are primates, which means we are related to the great apes. Our closest cousins are the chimpanzees. All of which I told you yesterday, and which you'd remember if you'd been paying attention. Now, class, open your history books to page thirty-four. The Pioneers. They crossed the Great Plains in covered wagons. Conditions were harsh. They had to hunt for their food."

A small red-haired boy wearing a shirt and tie waved politely from the desk next to Sally.

"Yes, Rodney?" asked Mr. Zukas. "Did you have a question?"

"Not a question, Mr. Zukas. Just a remark. It might interest the class to know that the Pioneers frequently ate deer as well as buffalo. They shot them with rifles."

Mr. Zukas beamed at him. "That's right, Rodney. I'm glad some-one's been doing their homework."

Rodney smirked proudly while behind him the rest of the class rolled their eyes.

"Can anyone else tell me what other animals the Pioneers might have hunted?" asked Mr. Zukas.

Sally waved furiously.

"Anyone at all?" Mr. Zukas asked somewhat desperately.

Sally bounced up and down in her seat, arm still waving.

Mr. Zukas sighed. "Yes, Sally."

"They ate gophers."

Loud expressions of disgust erupted from the rest of the class. Sally turned around and glared at them.

"I'm fairly certain the Pioneers didn't eat gophers, Sally," said Mr. Zukas. "I believe gophers are inedible."

"Nuh-uh," said Sally. "Gophers are super edible. The Pioneers roasted them over campfires and put hot sauce on them. They tasted like corn dogs. Only furry."

"Eeeww." The rest of the class unanimously decided it was

grossed out. Rodney cleared his throat and looked disdainfully at Sally.

"In the unlikely event that the Pioneers ate gophers," said Rodney with a sneer, "they would have skinned them first. The fur would have been removed before roasting."

"Nuh-uh," retorted Sally. "The fur's where all the vitamins are. Just like potatoes. You keep the skin on for the vitamins."

Behind Sally, Katie gasped and put her hand over her mouth. She had turned a sickly shade of green.

Mr. Zukas peered at her. "Katie, do you need to use the Little Girl's Room?"

Katie nodded tearfully at him. He waved impatiently in the direction of the door and Katie dashed out of the classroom.

Mr. Zukas sighed and turned a page in his textbook. "Let's get off the topic of the Pioneers' diet. Class, have a look at the picture on the next page. See the tin star this man is wearing? That meant he was a sheriff. He kept order in the lawless Wild West. Of course, it was a difficult job, and he needed lots of help. Frequently he would deputize. That means to create a kind of temporary sheriff. Who do you think he deputized?"

"Hamsters," said Sally at once.

Mr. Zukas pulled at his tie, looking like he was tempted to strangle himself with it. "Hamsters cannot be deputies or anything else in the law enforcement arena, Sally. Hamsters are furry rodents, just like gophers."

Sally's eyes flashed dangerously. "Hamsters are nothing like gophers! Hamsters and gophers are sworn enemies. Just ask my hamster, Melvin. You don't want to get him started on gophers. He gets so mad his fur stands straight up and he hops around like microwave popcorn. Besides, hamsters can so be in the law enforcement arena. Melvin is in the law enforcement arena. He's a Secret Agent. He has a Secret Agent JetPack and everything. He straps it on and flies around

San Francisco looking for bad guys. If he finds any bad guys he zaps them with his Secret Agent Laser Gun." Sally jumped up and aimed an imaginary laser gun at Mr. Zukas. "Kerpow!"

Mr. Zukas sighed and put a hand on his forehead. "Recess is early today," he said. "Everyone clear out of here. And stay out until the bell rings. I don't care if a tornado sweeps through the schoolyard. If anyone so much as puts one toe inside this classroom in the next half hour I'll personally feed them to the monster that lives in the school basement. He loves to snack on little kids. Especially ones who own hamsters."

"THERE HE IS. Charlie Sanderson, Snot Extraordinaire. Are you ready?" Sally was on the Jungle Gym, hanging upside down by her knees. One of her braids had come undone and her long hair was covering her face. She parted it with her hands and peered at a blond-haired boy walking past. He was wearing baggy pants, expensive sneakers, and a backwards baseball cap and was surrounded by a bunch of boys dressed exactly like him.

Katie peered up at Sally worriedly from a safe perch on the lowest bar of the Jungle Gym. She had her skirt neatly tucked under her legs and her shiny patent leather shoes were carefully resting on a clean patch of grass. "Ready for what?" she asked.

"The Plan," whispered Sally.

"You never told me the plan. I don't know what to do. You just said you had a Secret Revenge Plan, and that there were no Iguanas."

"That's right," said Sally. "We don't need an Iguana for this plan, which is a good thing because Arnold the Iguana is retiring from the revenge business. Arnold had a little chat with Melvin at one of their Secret Agent meetings in the school cafeteria. Arnold told Melvin that he was getting too old for Secret Revenge Plans. He's going to retire to a home for elderly Iguanas in Florida. They spend all day sleeping in hammocks and drinking chocolate milkshakes. Melvin tried to talk him out of it. Mel's afraid Arnold will get fat from all the chocolate milkshakes, but Arnold's already pretty fat because Emily Nieder-bacher keeps feeding him her peanut butter and jelly sandwiches." Sally grabbed the Jungle Gym bar with both hands, flipped her legs through and dropped to the ground. "We don't need Arnold for this particular Secret Revenge Plan. You can be my back up. Follow me."

Katie sighed and reluctantly followed Sally across the playground.

Sally swerved around a group of kids playing hopscotch and saun-tered in the direction of Charlie Sanderson and his posse, who were leaning against the schoolyard's chain-link fence and attempting to look cool. One of the boys nudged Charlie in the ribs and pointed at Sally.

Sally walked up to Charlie and slapped him on the back. "How's it going, Sanderson?"

The posse laughed and Charlie angrily pushed Sally away. "Get away from me, Hesslop, you freak."

Sally smiled. "I may be a freak, but you're a geek. And may I say, you really reek."

Charlie tried to shove her again, but Sally dodged away. She waved at Charlie as he and his posse stalked off to a far corner of the playground. Sally pulled something out of her pocket and tied it to the chain-link fence.

"What are you doing?" whispered Katie. "Are we going to get in trouble again? I can't go to the Principal's office again. I just can't. Mrs. Finsterman always says she's going to pinch my arm with that clothes pin she keeps on her desk."

"She won't pinch you," said Sally, watching the boys depart.

"How do you know? She always says she will."

"I know 'cause she always says she's going to pinch me too, but she never does. It's a psychotogical strategy, like when Xena pretend-ed to be a goddess and the Mud People worshipped her."

Katie stared at her in bafflement. "Mrs. Finsterman is a Mud Person?"

Sally put a finger to her mouth to shush Katie and pointed at the group of boys. Charlie and his gang were about twenty yards away, torturing a first-grader by throwing pebbles at him. The first-grader hopped around like a frightened puppy, not sure whether to cry or run.

Sally checked the fence and muttered to herself. "Two more feet. Come on, you poophead. Keep walking."

Katie frowned at her in confusion. She peered at the group of boys then bent down to examine the fence. "Sally, what . . ."

Sally waved her arms to shush her. The school bell rang, signaling the end of recess. Kids started running for the doors. Charlie Sanderson and his posse followed at a leisurely pace. Suddenly Charlie halted, frowning. He pulled at the waistline of his baggy pants, shrugged, and took another step. Sally yanked Katie away from the fence, giggling wildly. She ran into the school building, pulling Katie along behind her.

A huge burst of laughter suddenly erupted from the school yard. Sally stood on her tiptoes and peeked out of the glass window in the front door of the building. Charlie Sanderson was standing in the middle of the playground with his baggy pants down around his ankles and his Finding Nemo underpants on display for all to see. Kids pointed at him, wetting themselves from laughing. Grinning wickedly, Sally pulled a small piece of fishing line from her pocket and showed it to Katie.

Chapter Three

———◆●◆———

S ALLY WAS LYING on the floor of the Hesslop's living room, peering under an armchair. Muttering under her breath, she reached under the chair and pulled out a slinky and a blackened banana peel. Behind her, Robbie was sitting in the middle of the room wearing Snoopy underpants and his bike helmet. He giggled and whacked himself on the head with a toilet brush, matching the rhythm of Michael Jackson's Beat it, which was playing on the radio.

Sally sighed. The armchair was not delivering the goods. She crawled over to the sofa. Darlene Trockworthy was sitting there with her legs stretched out on the coffee table, painting her toenails. As she crawled under Darlene's legs Sally accidentally bumped them. A streak of Cotton Candy pink shot across Darlene's toes and up her ankle.

"Damn it, kid," groused Darlene, "Watch what you're doing. You made me mess up my pedicure."

"Sorry," Sally mumbled grudgingly. "It's just that I can't find Melvin. Have you seen him?"

"Nope, and good riddance," said Darlene. "That rodent's always creeping around underfoot. I swear he tries to trip me on purpose."

Sally sat back on her heels and smirked at Darlene. "He does that 'cause it's part of his Secret Mission. He's Special Agent Melvin, and he goes to Washington BC every weekend for Super Secret Hamster Orders. He's trained to trip all enemy combatants."

Darlene wiped the nail polish off her foot. "Well, if you can't find him maybe he's at the White House meeting the President," she said. "I hear they serve hamster every Friday."

Sally gave her an evil glare and flopped on her stomach to peer under the sofa.

Behind her Melvin suddenly appeared, rolling across the living room on an old-fashioned four-wheeled roller skate. His chubby rear-end didn't quite fit on the skate, and he dusted a path across the floor with his fur. He rolled from one end of the room to the other and disappeared into the kitchen. Robbie waved the toilet brush at him as he passed.

Sally pulled her head out from under the sofa and hopped to her feet. She planted her fists on her hips. "Drat you, Melvin. Where are you? If you're hiding in the microwave again I'm going to spank your little furry butt. You know Dad hates it when his microwave popcorn tastes like hamster."

She stomped into the kitchen and opened the microwave. No Melvin. She banged open cupboards and rattled pans. "Melvin, if you've gone on a Secret Mission again you are soooo in trouble. You know you aren't supposed to go on Secret Missions after your bedtime. I'm gonna write to Washington. They'll remote you back to Janitor Melvin and take away your Secret Agent Jetpack."

Sally crawled under the kitchen table and peered inside an empty box of Wheaties. Behind her Melvin had managed (by methods known only to himself and other Secret Agent Hamsters) to get himself on top of the fridge. He poked his nose over the side and surveyed the perilous drop to the kitchen counter. After a moment's hesitation, he stepped off the fridge, executing a perfect swan dive with a half-twist. He landed face-first on the kitchen counter then slowly toppled over onto his back, legs in the air. He tried to roll onto his feet but was hampered by a touch of middle-aged spread. After several tries he got himself right-side up and waddled to the edge of the countertop. At that moment Robbie wandered in, fencing with his toilet brush. Melvin took a step into the unknown and landed splat on top of Robbie's bike helmet, all four feet splayed out and hanging on for dear life. Oblivious to his stowaway, Robbie fenced back into the living room, taking Melvin with him.

"Sally, get off the floor," said Mr. Hesslop as he entered the kitchen, a pencil behind his ear and the grumpy look of a man who's just been wrestling with his tax returns. "You're as bad as Robbie. Remember, you're supposed to set a good example for him. Now, go brush your teeth. It's bedtime."

Sally scrambled out from under the table and saluted. "Sir. Yes Sir. Your orders we obey. We're here to save the day. Good dental hygiene is a must. We'll clean our teeth or bust." She marched out of the kitchen, humming a martial tune. At the end of the hall she pivoted sharply and entered a small bathroom whose plumbing fixtures dated from the fifties. A bulging hamper full of wet towels sat in the corner and a flotilla of rubber ducks was lined up along the edge of the bathtub. The back of the toilet overflowed with half-empty shampoo bottles.

Sally knelt and began throwing towels out of the hamper. "Melvin, you varmint, you're about to become a garment. My Xena doll needs a fur coat, and you've got my vote."

She stuck her head into the now empty hamper. Behind her Melvin sauntered into the bathroom and scrambled up onto the edge of the tub, climbing the pyramid of wet towels Sally had dumped on the floor. He wound his way along the rim of the bathtub, which was full of soapy water leftover from Robbie's bath. Melvin dodged the rubber ducks with surprising agility, but overconfidence got the better of him and he slipped, falling into the bathtub with a splash.

Sally pulled her head out of the hamper and rushed over. "Melvin, you poophead. Your Secret Agent Swimming Lessons aren't til next week."

A stream of bubbles floating up from under the water was the only answer. Sally scooped Melvin up and deposited him on the bathroom rug. Melvin shook like a tiny dog and sat shivering, his orange fur matted to his sides.

"It's okay, Mel," said Sally. "I'll fix you right up with my Top Secret Air Blaster."

She grabbed a blow drier and turned it on High. The blast of hot air rolled Melvin over backward. He did a full somersault and ended up on standing on his head against the side of the bathtub. Sally picked him up and aimed the blow drier at his tummy. His fur blew straight backward as if he was in a hurricane. When Sally had finished drying him he was twice his normal size and had the hamster version of an Afro.

"Melvin! That's a great disguise. You can use it on your next un-dercover mission. Nobody will ever recognize you. You can be Horace the Hairdresser, famous for your skills with a curling iron. All the lady hamsters will be lining up to make an appointment with you."

Melvin's Afro started to deflate.

"Hang on Melvin," said Sally. "You just need some Product to maintain volume. That's what those hair commercials on TV are always saying."

Sally grabbed a can of hair mousse from the cabinet under the sink and sprayed a big glob on Melvin, who promptly disappeared under a pile of foam. Sally dug him out of the foam and rubbed the mousse into his fur, then snatched a toothbrush from the sink. "This is Dad's. He won't mind," said Sally as she brushed Melvin's fur into spikes. She sat him back down on the bathroom rug.

"There! You totally look like a cool dude. You look like one of those singers on American Idol. You just need to learn how to dance."

Sally jumped up and launched into a wild dance step. Melvin backed into a corner as Sally's flailing arms whacked the shower curtain and knocked a shampoo bottle into the toilet. Sally finished with a flourish and bowed low before an imaginary audience. "C'mon Mel. It's not hard. You just do little wiggle and a little rap. You just gotta have attitude. Like this."

Sally grabbed a rubber duck and sang into it like a microphone. "My name's Sally J. and I'm here to say, I'm doing my dance 'cause I pulled down Charlie's pants."

Sally picked up Melvin and danced around with him. "You need a hamster rap. All the tough hamsters have one. And maybe some bling. I wonder if Dad would buy you a gold chain."

Melvin looked decidedly skeptical about this, not to mention sea-sick from all the dancing.

Sally danced into her bedroom, singing. "I'm furry and I'm cute. I'm a Secret Agent to boot. I've got a special JetPack which is totally wack."

She tucked Melvin into his Hamster Habitat. Melvin trundled down the orange tube to his usual nest, his sticky moussed fur attracting bits of sawdust. By the time he reached his nest in the middle of the Habitat he looked like a tiny pile of kindling.

"Another super disguise, Mel," said Sally. "Totally cool. You can do your next Secret Mission at Tony's Pizza. They have sawdust all over their floor. They'll never spot you. You can sneak into the kitchen and find out the ingredients of their Secret Pizza Sauce."

Melvin burrowed into the sawdust of his nest until he was just a sawdust-lump. Sally yawned and blew him a kiss. "Night Mel."

Chapter Four

"SALLY JANE HESSLOP, you are a demon spawn."

Mrs. Patterson, leader of Girl Scout Troop 112, wiped the milk off her sour face and glared down at Sally. The two of them were faced off in the middle of the Montgomery Elementary School cafeteria. A table with cartons of milk and a plate of Rice Krispie Treats was setup in one corner.

The wayward milk had ended up on Mrs. Patterson's face through totally unavoidable circumstances. Sally had been chasing another Girl Scout while holding a carton of milk and a straw. Squirting had been inevitable.

Sally planted her fists on her hips and regaled Mrs. Patterson with a cold stare. They were old enemies. They had disliked each other from the very first day that Mrs. Patterson had assumed the leadership of the troop. On that fateful day Sally had been showing the other Girl Scouts how to slide along the newly polished wooden floor in their stocking feet. She had just launched into a particularly energetic slide when Mrs. Patterson had walked through the door of the cafeteria. The resulting collision had knocked Mrs. Patterson off her feet and onto her support-hose covered knees. Mrs. Patterson had been trying to transfer Sally to another Girl Scout troop ever since, so far without success.

"Well," said Sally, "if I'm a demon spawn then I bet it's a cool demon, one that can shoot flames out of its eyeballs. I wish I could shoot flames out of my eyeballs. I'd turn Charlie Sanderson into a crispy critter."

Mrs. Patterson raised her eyes to the heavens. "When I say that you are a demon spawn, Sally Jane Hesslop, it means that you are a very bad girl. One of the worst I've had the misfortune to meet in all my years of guiding Girl Scouts along the difficult path to becoming young ladies."

Sally fiddled with her straw. "I'd rather be a demon spawn than a young lady. I bet demon spawn have cool super powers. The coolest super power would be to turn people into potato bugs. My first victim would be Charlie Sanderson. If I turned him into a potato bug it would be a big improvement. I'd probably get a medal from the President. Then they'd have a parade for me and I'd ride on a float past the White House and wave to the crowd. Like this." Sally energetically waved her arms, spraying drops of milk onto Mrs. Patterson's bouffant hairdo.

Mrs. Patterson closed her eyes and kneaded her forehead with two shaking fingers. "Sally Jane Hesslop, we were discussing you spewing milk everywhere and making a mess, not super powers and potato bugs. Now go get some paper towels from the restroom and wipe this up."

"Okay" said Sally, shrugging. She tucked the straw under her Girl Scout beanie. "When do we get to make bird feeders from pinecones? That's in the Girl Scout handbook, you know. Page forty-nine. You stick peanut butter in the pinecones so the birds can peck it out. Though I don't understand why we can't just spread the peanut butter on Ritz crackers. Then the birds could peck it real easy. Molly Sanderson says it's because the birds like to work hard for their food, but that's just stupid. Besides, Molly is Charlie Sanderson's sister and she picks her nose, so you know anything she says is suspected. That's what my Dad says. Nose pickers are Dim Bulbs and to be suspected. The crackers don't have to be Ritz. Wheat Thins would work good too."

Mrs. Patterson sighed. "Sally Jane Hesslop, I don't know what you're blathering on about. Get this mess cleaned up. Now."

Mindy Nichols, a thin black girl with red bows on the ends of her cornrows, ran up to Sally. She peered after the departing Mrs. Patterson with a fearful expression. "Sally, guess what? Mrs. Osterman isn't coming today. She's in the hospital."

Mrs. Osterman was the co-leader of the troop. She was a quiet young woman with a warm smile who was liked by all the Girl Scouts.

"You mean it's just us and Prissy Patterson?" groaned Sally. "Oh barf. Why is Mrs. Osterman in the hospital?"

"Molly Sanderson says it's because she's having an operation," whispered Mindy.

Sally rolled her eyes. "Molly is always saying stupid stuff. You know that. She's a Sanderson. You can't believe anything she says. C'mon. Let's go ask Sandra Chang. She'll know."

Sally and Mindy ran up to a group of girls gathered around Sandra Chang, a tall, graceful Chinese girl with a curtain of shiny black hair hanging all the way to her hips. A purple silk scarf was artfully tied around the neck of her Girl Scout uniform.

Sally barged her way through the group. "Hey Sandra."

Sandra nodded at her graciously, like a benevolent Queen acknowledging her subjects.

"Sandra, what's up with Mrs. Osterman? Mindy says she's in the hospital."

"I'm sorry, Sally," replied Sandra Chang in a quiet, authoritative voice. "I don't know the details. All I know is that Mrs. Patterson is taking over as Troop Leader."

Loud groans erupted from all the Girl Scouts within earshot. Molly Sanderson, a short, pudgy blond girl with two front teeth missing, sister to the infamous Charlie Sanderson, jumped up and down frantically, waving her hand as if in school.

"Thandra. Thandra," lisped Molly, "I know what'th happened to Mrs. Othterman. My brother Charlie told me."

On hearing Charlie's name Sally made loud gagging noises and clutched her throat. Molly ignored her, looking intently at Sandra. Finally Sandra gave her a regal nod.

"Mrs. Othterman ith having a Hystertology," whispered Molly excitedly. "That'th an operation. It meanth thee can't have babiesth anymore, unlesth she goeth to Mexico and getsth it reverthed. Then her babiesth will come out backwardsth, like when your Dad backth the car out of the garage. Latht week my Dad backed our car out of the garage and ran over my brother'th bicycle. My Dad said a very bad wordth."

Sally planted her hands on her hips and gave Molly a look of scathing contempt. "That's not a Hystertology, Sanderson. A Hystertology is when you have your ears pinned back. The doctor staples them to your head so you don't look like Dumbo."

"Mrs. Othterman doesthn't look like Dumbo," said Molly.

"Well, not anymore," shot back Sally. "She's had a Hystertology. Sheesh, Sanderson. You are such a dimwit sometimes. I guess it runs in the family."

Molly advanced on her, fists clenched. "You take that back Hessthlop."

Sally assumed a Xena fighting pose. "C'mon, Sanderson. I'll lick you, and then I'll go lick your stupid brother."

"Charlie's a twit,

He's Molly's brother.

He has half a wit,

Molly has the other."

Sally raised her leg in preparation for a super-duper martial arts kick. Molly stood her ground for a second, then thought better of it and dashed off to find Mrs. Patterson.

"Girls! Girls!" shouted Mrs. Patterson from the center of the cafeteria. "Everyone gather round. It's Share Time. Bring the item you're going to share with the group over here."

There was a noisy scramble as all the Girl Scouts rushed to a pile of backpacks stacked against the wall, and then convened in the center of the room. They threw themselves on the wooden floor in a cross-legged circle around Mrs. Patterson.

"Molly, dear, why don't you go first," said Mrs. Patterson.

Molly Sanderson smirked at the others and walked to the center of the circle. She held up a Barbie doll dressed in an immaculate princess-type costume of white silk with a red velvet cape. "Thith ith Princeth Thophie of Bavaria. Thee's dressthed for the ball. Thee's a Spethial Edition. My Mom bought her for me in New York at Bloomingdaleth."

"She's just beautiful, Molly," said Mrs. Patterson. "So precious. I bet all the young ladies here want to be Princesses, don't you, girls?"

Sally sprang up. "Of course. I'm Princess Scary Fighting Eagle from the Moping Moose tribe. We get dressed for balls too. We paint our faces with red stripes, stick eagle feathers in our ears, and do our Special Moose Waltz around the campfire."

Sally launched into a fast-paced dance, shaking her arms and kicking her legs over her head. Her beanie flew off, and girls scrambled backwards as she lunged wildly toward them. She concluded by spinning rapidly in a circle, then staggered dizzily back to her spot on the floor.

Mrs. Patterson closed her eyes during this performance. After Sally had sat down again she opened her eyes, a pained expression on her face. "Mindy," she sighed, "why don't you go next?"

Mindy Nichols moved to the center of the circle, bashfully pulling at her cornrows. She pulled a brightly colored paper bird from a bag. Several of the Girl Scouts oohed and aahed. Mindy smiled gratefully.

"This is a Japanese art called Origami. My Mom learned it when she was stationed at a Navy base in Sasebo, Japan. She taught it to me. This is a tsuru. That's Japanese for crane. All the kids in Japan learn to make them. The crane is a symbol of peace." Mindy sat down abruptly, looking embarrassed. The scouts applauded.

Mrs. Patterson pursed her lips as if she'd just drunk lemon juice. "Very, er, multi-cultural, Mindy. Though maybe you should bring something a little more American next time. These exotic things aren't really appropriate for Girl Scout meetings. Let's see, Sandra, why don't you come up."

Sandra Chang nodded and rose gracefully to her feet. She unrolled a paper scroll which displayed a vertical line of beautiful Chinese characters. "This is called calligraphy. It's a very popular art in China. These characters are in the Mandarin language, which my mother and grandmother speak. My grandmother taught me how to do calligraphy. We use a pot of black ink and a brush made of sheep's hair."

Sandra sat down and the Girl Scouts applauded respectfully.

"My goodness," said Mrs. Patterson, "This is certainly an international group. I feel like I'm at the United Nations. Well, onward. Who'd like to volunteer?"

Sally waved her arm wildly. Another scout across from Sally dared to raise her arm as well. Sally glared daggers at her opponent, and the offending scout promptly dropped her challenge and looked like she'd be thrilled to sink into the floor. Mrs. Patterson tried mightily to avoid Sally's gaze, but resistance was futile. Sally marched unbidden to the center of the circle, carrying a paper takeout carton. Mrs. Patterson raised her eyes heavenward.

"I'll go next, Mrs. Patterson," said Sally. She opened the carton and pulled out something wriggly. The Girl Scouts gasped in horror and the ones closest scooted away. Molly Sanderson screamed.

"Mrsth. Patterthon, Thally'th brought a rat! Eeeuww. Make her take ith away!"

Sally rolled her eyes. "It's not a rat, Sanderson, you doofus. It's my hamster, Melvin. My Dad shaved him. See, what happened was, I put some of Darlene Trockworthy's Super Hold Hair Mousse on him. Darlene wants to be my Dad's girlfriend, and she left her hair mousse in our bathroom."

Mrs. Patterson clutched the pearls around her neck and muttered something about tramps.

"Anyway," continued Sally, "it turns out you should never mousse a hamster. It glues their fur up something awful. Plus you should especially never put mousse on your hamster and then let him roll around in sawdust. My Dad said there must have been some kind of chemical reaction between the pine sap in the sawdust and Darlene's Super Hold Hair Mousse. It hardened up like that shellac stuff we used on our birdhouses last year. Poor Mel here couldn't even walk. He just rolled around like a pinecone with feet. So my Dad used his electric razor and shaved off all of Melvin's fur. So now Mel's got a crew cut, like an Army guy. Anybody want to hold him?"

The scouts all recoiled. Melvin dove back into the takeout container as Mrs. Patterson stepped forward and made shooing motions at Sally. Sally reluctantly relinquished center stage and sat back down. She dropped a Rice Krispie Treat into the takeout carton. "It's okay, Mel," she whispered into the carton, "Don't mind Prissy Patterson. The troop loved you. You were a big hit."

End of Excerpt

Made in the USA
Middletown, DE
16 June 2019